Book 6 of Morna's Legacy Series

Love Beyond Dreams

A Scottish Time Travel Romance

Bethany Claire

BCB

License Notes

Editor: Dj Hendrickson
Cover Designer: Damonza

Available In eBook & Paperback

eBook ISBN: 978-0-9960037-9-7
Paperback ISBN: 978-0-9961136-0-1

http://www.bethanyclaire.com

For Dad

Chapter 1

Cagair Castle—Present Day

Eyes are the most important part of any portrait. People may not notice if you goof up a chin or if the shape of their nose isn't just so, but they will always notice if you get the eyes wrong.

My very first art teacher told me that—the eccentric old woman with a slight hoarding problem that my parents hired to teach me when I was no more than eight. I never liked the idea of so much pressure being placed on a piece of art, so I took to painting landscapes, abstracts, anything that didn't require me replicating the image of another person with paint and a brush.

Besides, I don't have any real talent for portraits, or so I thought, but looking at the painting of the stranger in front of me made me think differently. Of course, I wasn't sure talent had anything to do with the way this painting turned out. The image of my stranger was so burned into my mind that I believe I could paint him just as well even if I'd never held a brush in my life.

This man—with his dark hair and eyes so blue they looked like they were made of stained glass—was the most beautiful thing I'd ever created. I wanted nothing more than for him to crawl right out of the canvas and into my bedroom.

Maybe now that I'd placed him onto something that would last for longer than the duration of my dreams, he would stop haunting me in my sleep.

All that remained was for me to add my signature to the bottom then the painting would be complete and maybe, just maybe, I could have a night's sleep without him invading every corner of my mind.

"Ye will run out of socks if he keeps that up."

It took the sound of Aiden's voice behind me to draw my attention to the needle-like teeth that nipped at my big toe as Toby pulled at my sock in an effort to yank me off my stool. I sat the brush down after my final stroke and leaned down to scoop the young pup into my arms before turning to face him.

Aiden stood tall and gangly in the doorway, his friendly, dimpled smile a welcome sight after my hours spent alone in the tower. Usually he was covered in sawdust, but he cleaned up nicely, albeit casually, with his longish blonde hair pulled into a small ponytail at the nape of his neck and bare toes sticking out underneath the bottom of his jeans. He had spent his entire life in Scotland, but at first sight I would have sworn he was a native Californian.

"I already have. I'm pretty sure every other pair already has a hole. I should really start wearing shoes. I just hate them so much."

Aiden laughed and came over to rub Toby behind the ears before pointing to the painting. "Me as well. Is that the likeness of yer boyfriend?"

I stood and moved to stand next to Aiden, setting Toby on the ground as I did so.

"No, unfortunately, it isn't."

Aiden crossed his arms and tilted his head as he grinned mischievously at me. "Best not show him this then."

I laughed and swatted his arm playfully. "Aiden, I don't have a boyfriend. Don't you think if I did, you would have heard something about it by now? We've spent pretty much every day together for the last six months."

"Wrong answer."

My confusion grew with each new word. "What are you talking about?"

"Gillian, I knew that ye dinna have a boyfriend, or at least I dinna think that ye did. If ye did, I'd say he was a sorry arse of a man for ye havena seen him in the last six months. Billy asked me if ye had one, ye see. I told him aye, to save ye the misery of having the man try to woo ye."

I picked up Toby and handed him over to Aiden then went about cleaning up my mess.

"Woo me? Billy has never said three words to me. I can't imagine how he'd ever work up the nerve to do that."

"Oh, ye'd be surprised. A drink or two and he will talk yer ear off. Ye wouldna like it. Trust me."

"Oh, I do. What are you doing up here? Are you already done for the day?"

"Aye, I've sent all the men home. Anne has a special weekend planned for our anniversary. We will be away, but I'll have my phone if ye or Tracy need me."

"I haven't heard from Tracy in three months. I'll be shocked if you hear from her this weekend."

My sister, Tracy, didn't need anyone except her husband, Mark. And even with him, if she ever had to choose between him or his bank accounts, I knew without question which one she would choose.

"Aye, well, I doona expect to hear from her but if she tries, I'll have my phone." He gestured toward the painting. "Is this a piece of work that has been commissioned?"

"No." I bit the corner of my lip as I paused my cleaning and reached to grab onto my thinnest brush as I dipped it into black paint before quickly scribbling my signature on the bottom. "This one's just for me."

"Just for ye, eh?" He raised his brow and nodded teasingly.

I laughed and resumed cleaning my brushes, ignoring him.

"So why did ye paint this man? Do ye know him?"

I shook my head. "No, I don't know him. I'm not even sure if he's real. It's the strangest thing. Every night, and I mean every single night since I've been here, I've dreamt about him."

Aiden's eyes widened as he nodded his head knowingly. "Have ye now? Ye know this castle has quite a history. Perhaps he is one of the ghosts that roam these halls."

I shrugged. "Maybe, but I've been here for months, and I've not seen any ghosts."

"Neither have I, but other things have happened. The lassies that owned the castle before yer sister bought it vanished no more than a month after buying the place, and that is no the only strange occurrence to take place here."

It was the first I'd heard of anything like that, but it went a long way toward explaining why Tracy purchased the castle in the first place. "Well, that's probably the reason Tracy bought it. She loves stuff like that—anything that screams of adventure.

Although, she never loves anything enough to stick with it, hence my being here to watch over you and Toby."

Aiden pointed to the pup now sleeping soundly in his arms.

"It will be hard for ye to give him back to her when she returns, aye?"

"Oh, that's so not happening. She had him a whole three days before I got here to watch him and the castle. He's known me way longer than he knew her. Toby's my dog now."

Aiden nodded then, seeing I was finished cleaning, stepped toward the doorway before we walked down the spiral steps together.

"As he should be. I've known Tracy a long time, but even I canna believe how little time she's spent here. She's no approved most of the work. What if she doesna like all I've done?"

My sister and I were as different as night and day, but even she couldn't deny the good that Aiden and his men had done to this place. They had breathed life back into a structure that had needed it for so long.

"I doubt it. All she wants is for you to restore the property with as much historical accuracy as you can. You have more than enough consultants helping with that so I'm sure she will be very pleased. How could she not be? I can't believe how much you've accomplished so quickly. It's gorgeous."

"I've no done it alone. I've had help."

He had, but the rest were just hired workers that came in and out in however many days it took them to complete their specific job. Aiden had put everything into the castle, even moving him and his wife into it so he could devote his time to the castle's restoration around the clock.

"Maybe so, but none of them have worked as hard as you have. You really have a love for this place. I can see it in the way you care for it. It's what this place has needed for centuries."

"Aye, I do. As do ye. Tracy shouldna own a place like this. I know she willna keep it. If I had the funds, I'd buy it from her in a minute."

Of course she planned to sell it. Tracy and Mark never stayed in any place for more than a few months. His endless supply of money earned through some sort of self-made internet business—I couldn't begin to tell you what he actually did for a living—afforded them the sort of lifestyle that allowed them to do exactly what they wanted whenever they felt like it. They took full advantage, never taking anyone or anything else into consideration when making their decisions.

I was truly flabbergasted the day Tracy called to tell me she'd bought the place, even more so when she called me three weeks later saying they were headed to Japan for something related to Mark's business. Naturally, she wanted me, the artist who could work from anywhere, to come and oversee the renovations.

Tracy didn't make commitments. She and Mark didn't own a home. They didn't have children. As far as I knew, they didn't even have a consistent place to pick up their mail. Then suddenly, within a month, she purchased a castle, adopted a puppy, and passed both ginormous responsibilities over to me.

Not that I overly minded really. How could I complain when I'd been able to spend the last six months in a gorgeous castle painting in a storybook-like tower and my evenings cuddling the fluffiest puppy I'd ever seen?

"You're right. I'm certain she has no intention of staying here. You're old friends though. Maybe you can talk her down on the price and buy it like you said?"

"If it were only Tracy, I might convince her, but Mark has his money for a reason. He willna accept a penny less than what it's worth. It's a shame. Cagair needs someone who loves it to stay and care for it—to live in it."

"Yes, it does." I motioned my head toward the door. "Are you about to head out?"

"Aye, I just thought I'd come and tell ye goodbye. I'll see ye on Monday. Will ye be all right here all by yerself?"

I stood with him in the foyer and glanced around at the beautiful stones and soft lights installed to modernize the place in a way that made it functional for future generations. I loved everything about this castle. I would be more than okay staying here by myself. I would love every minute of it.

"Absolutely. You two go and have a great time."

Chapter 2

The Caves Near Cagair Castle—1649

Marion thought the waves should frighten him, should serve as a fierce reminder of how close he'd come to losing his life so many moons ago. They didn't, for he couldn't bring himself to be scared of something he didn't remember. Instead, he found the water to be a balm to his sore skin and soul—a place where he felt most at home in a world that now seemed so unfamiliar. His arms moved with ease, his head lifting and falling as he breathed in the wet, salty air. He only allowed himself a few moments in the water each day, and he reveled in them. For there among the waves, he didn't have to try to remember everything that he could not.

He didn't remember his fall into the water or the slight but strong arms of Marion who pulled his seemingly lifeless body off the shore and into her cave. The days and weeks following were a haze of pain and messy dreams, but all of that seemed so far away now.

His bones were now healed, his skin scarred but no longer open, and his mind was as whole as he imagined it would ever be. He could remember nothing before Marion's hands found him at the water's edge, and the loss of himself remained a constant torment to his mind.

What if he had family or friends who cared for him, that thought him dead or missing? He hated the thought that his broken mind might keep those he loved but no longer knew in a state of endless grief.

He dressed quickly after his swim and made the short walk to where he fished each day. Despite the loss of his memories, his skills remained. He could catch fish in half the time it took Marion to do the same task. They planned to meet on the rocks so that he could start teaching her the proper way to fish. He wondered how she survived for so long on her own with the way she did it, bouncing and lashing down at the water like some sort of forest bear. He needed to begin working with her soon. It would take time to improve her skills, and he couldn't stay here forever.

He smiled when he saw her. Her dark black hair, wild and tangled, blew in the wind around her face as she held up a hand to block the sun. From such a distance, Marion looked much younger than she did up close. He couldn't help but wonder how old she really was. Her gentle mannerisms made her seem young, but the deep lines in her face aged her considerably.

Not that it mattered, he knew even less about her than she did of him, and that suited them both just fine. It made theirs an easy sort of friendship. He would forever be grateful to her for saving his life. He only hoped that she would understand his need to leave here.

He wasn't sure she could see him with the sun blinding her eyes, but he knew when she spoke that she could at least hear him approaching.

"Craig, what took ye so long? Did ye swim to the other side of the ocean and back?"

There were times, brief and fleeting, when something would pull at some lost corner of a memory. Each time Marion called him Craig was one of those. While he didn't know what his name was, he knew it wasn't Craig. He had to remind himself to reply to the name each and every time.

"'Tis no my name, Marion. And it dinna take me any longer than usual. 'Tis only that ye are no usually about here waiting for me to finish."

Marion nodded and stood. He knew she was ready to begin the lesson.

"True enough, but doona tell me no to call ye Craig. Until the day ye are able to tell me yer real name, 'tis what I shall call ye. For it means 'rocks' and 'twas the rocks from which ye fell."

He'd spent every day since he was strong enough to walk looking up at the perilous rocks leading to Cagair Castle. He couldn't imagine how anyone could survive such a fall, but Marion swore that was when she first saw him—tumbling from the rocks that lay far above them, crashing into the ocean before he washed ashore at her feet.

"Are ye ready for me to show ye how to fish so ye can catch enough to feed yerself without me?"

She looked squarely at him, crossed both arms, and sat back down on the rocks before motioning for him to do the same. "No. We willna be fishing this day. Come and sit next to me, Craig."

"Ye dinna need to say that name right then, Marion. I know at times ye must say the name ye have given me to get my attention, but ye could have just ended after saying, 'come and sit next to me.' Ye dinna have to say 'Craig.'"

She smiled and nudged him as he sat next to her. "Aye, I know it."

He waited for her to finish laughing before speaking again. "Now, what do ye mean we willna be fishing this day? I've spent enough days with ye to know that ye willna be willing to go without eating."

"Ye are right, I willna go without eating. I've already caught three fish all on my own, and I fed myself for many years before ye came along. Yer way might be better, but mine works just fine for me."

"Mayhap so, but I'd still like to teach ye during the time I have left here."

"And just how much time to do ye think that might be?"

He shrugged, hoping that his answer wouldn't upset her. Guilt always filled him when he thought about leaving Marion, but he couldn't stay with her. If his memories didn't return, he had to start anew in whatever way he could. He didn't wish for the sort of solitude Marion seemed to crave.

"Two moons, no more."

Her snort took him aback.

"Two moons? Ye plan to stay that long? I've spent more time with ye than I have another person in years, and I doona care for it. Ye no longer need time or help to heal. 'Tis time that ye prepare to leave me here."

It wasn't the reaction he expected from her, but he couldn't help but be relieved that Marion wouldn't be sad to see him go. She was the only friend he had, the only person he knew at all. He didn't want to cause her pain in any way but as he was learning more and more, loneliness seemed to suit the strange, cave-dwelling wildling.

"If ye think it best, I can leave come morning."

"Aye, I do. 'Tis time for us to part ways, ye and I. Being near ye has stirred feelings that I had for others long ago. They are best left forgotten."

It was the most sentimental statement he'd ever heard from her, and he wondered if perhaps he'd already stayed longer than he should have.

"Marion," he glanced over at her. The sadness in her eyes took him aback. He reached for her hand before he thought better of it. She flinched away from him, but he continued with his question. "Why doona ye come with me? Leave this place and start a life anew for yerself? I doona know what happened in yer life to cause ye to seek such solitude, but ye doona have to remain in it. We could venture out together."

She pushed herself up from the rocks, bent to gather the fish she'd caught on her own, and turned away from him before speaking.

"No. I've no desire for that. Ye will leave on yer own come morning. Climb to the top of the rocks tonight, and cross the bridge into the village so that ye might decide where ye wish to start out tomorrow. I never see anyone about the castle. Ye should be able to cross the castle grounds unnoticed."

He already knew that. He'd spent many evenings making his way to the top of the island where the castle lay, taking long walks in the moonlight around its grounds. He'd not yet dared to cross the bridge leading to the village, but it seemed that tonight Marion was giving him no choice but to do just that.

It was time for his life to start all over again.

Chapter 3

Cagair Castle—Present Day

I enjoyed my weekend alone in the castle with Toby. I really had, but regardless of how much I reveled in being able to stay in my pajamas until noon and take multiple bubble baths a day, I still found myself quite ready for Aiden, Anne, and the rest of the construction crew to return when Monday morning arrived.

At first, when nobody showed up, I assumed their travel had been somehow delayed and Aiden didn't want his men to start work without him. Despite my disappointment, I didn't worry about them overmuch and went about my normal weekday routine.

I walked Toby, showered, dressed, ate some breakfast, and went to painting rather aimlessly at a blank piece of canvas. Before I knew it, the day slipped away, as it often did when I was painting. It wasn't until Toby finally lost his patience and sunk his sharp, needle-like teeth into my foot in an effort to get me to stop and play that I glanced up to see that the sun had already started its descent.

Aiden still hadn't arrived, and that realization made me worry. He wasn't the sort of person to not call when plans changed.

Needing to alleviate my paranoia that something terrible had happened to him, I pulled Toby away from my foot and into my arms before taking out my phone to give him a call. When there was no answer, I left him a short message before setting Toby back on the ground so that I could quickly clean up my mess as I rationalized all of the possible reasons for his absence.

Perhaps they'd decided to extend their weekend getaway, or he'd lost his cell phone. There were a great many logical possibilities so I resolved myself to letting go of any worry before it was absolutely necessary.

Toby would help me with that, as he continued to make it very clear that he'd spent enough time waiting for me to finish my work. I had to give the little guy some credit. He dutifully slept or bounced around at my feet all day while I worked, but now, an hour away from sunset, he started to demand that we get outdoors for at least part of the day. I couldn't blame him at all.

I looked down at him and smiled. Toby knew, after spending so many months with me, that this particular lift of the corner of my mouth signaled the end of my work and the start of him getting some real attention. He began running around the room like a mad man, spinning in circles around my feet and doing a pretty effective job at herding me out of the tower room.

The pup ran down the steps in front of me, stopping and pausing at each landing as he waited for me to catch up. The moment I reached him, he would take off once again. When we were finally down the stairs, I looked at him as I always did and pointed one finger at each end of the castle.

"Which is it today, Toby? The front or the back."

The front, as Toby knew, meant a nice long walk around the front grounds of the castle; the back, a game of fetch. He barked and took off toward the front door.

"A walk it is then."

I laughed and paused by the front door to slip on my shoes before reaching for the handle. When I pulled the door open, I looked down expecting Toby to run ahead of me at full speed. Instead, he walked slowly out the door while wagging his tail rapidly before he stopped and sniffed at a pair of tiny shoes standing just outside the doorway. I'd been so focused on Toby that I didn't notice the boy until I saw his shoes.

"Well, hello. Did you knock? I am so sorry. I've been upstairs working so I didn't hear you if you did. Can I help you with something?"

Only then, as I looked up from his shoes and into his face, did I notice that he carried a large suitcase in one hand.

"Hi there. Is it okay if I come in? This bag is awfully heavy. I packed a bunch of my dinosaurs to play with. I don't get to play with them much at home 'cause people start asking questions and then I get kinda tongue-tied."

Baffled, I leaned my head out of the doorway to see if any sort of parental figure appeared to be accompanying him. When I saw no one, I stepped aside and allowed him to enter. Cagair Castle wasn't the sort of place someone just walked up to accidentally. He didn't have the wrong address. If he was here, there was a reason for it, but as I watched him walk inside, I didn't have the slightest idea what it could be.

I tried to keep my expression approachable, but I could feel how tightly my brows were pinched. The child acted like I should be expecting him, when in truth, I'd never been more confused by anything in my entire life.

"Why would people question you for playing with your toys? Don't most kids do that?"

His eyes widened like I'd caught him in a lie, and he sat the suitcase down almost immediately before extending his little hand toward me. He looked up at me with beautiful green eyes, long, dark lashes that made me envious, and a smattering of adorable freckles across his cheeks. I smiled and took his hand gladly.

"See? Just like that. I'm a good thinker. Everybody says so, but sometimes, I just can't keep up with all the craziness and I say something that brings on the questions. Just never mind about the dinosaurs. My name is Cooper, we're here to rent the castle."

"You're here to rent the castle?" I reached for my phone on instinct, immediately suspecting that I would find some sort of last minute message from Tracy. It would be just like her to plan something like this without telling me. Still, the castle wasn't finished and although she hadn't seen it herself, Tracy knew that it would be months before Aiden's construction crew no longer lingered around the castle finishing their work. I couldn't imagine her renting the place out to guests before it reached completion.

"Um...yeah, aren't you Trisha or Tracy or Tiffany? I don't remember for sure, but I know Aunt Jane said she'd talked to somebody whose name started with a *T*."

As if she'd heard the boy's reference to her, my phone buzzed and Tracy's number displayed on the screen as I looked down at it. I swiped to answer, told her to hold on a tad bit too sharply, and then turned to speak to the young boy once again.

"Do you think you could wait here for me for just a moment? It's Tracy, the woman you were just talking about. I'm Gillian, her sister. Cooper, are your mom and dad around somewhere?"

He nodded and pointed outside. "Oh yeah. Well my mom and E-o are and my Aunt Jane and Uncle Adwen. They're just walking down the bridge from where the cars dropped us all off. They'll be here soon."

"Why did someone drop you off before the bridge? They could have driven down here."

"Oh." The boy shrugged. "Well, I think they just wanted to walk. I ran ahead of them."

I didn't believe him. The words fell out of his mouth awkwardly, and he looked uncomfortable and guilty.

"With their luggage?"

Cooper didn't respond. If not for Tracy's screeching voice coming through the phone asking where I was, I would've taken a step outside to watch for his supposed party and pressed him further. Instead, I just nodded and turned to walk halfway up the stairs so I could speak more privately to my sister. When I was close enough that I could still see the boy but far enough away that I didn't think he could hear me without straining, I spoke into the phone.

"You rented out the castle, Tracy? Aiden's not going to be pleased with that at all. He still has so many workers around here on most days and there's still a lot that they haven't finished."

"Oh, Gillie." She sounded completely unapologetic, as always. She could never see when she did something inconsiderate. “Aiden already knows. I talked to Anne a few hours ago. As soon as his drugs wear off, I’m sure he will be as thrilled as you will be about it once you hear how much they offered to pay me. She’s driving him back to the castle now. I’m sure you will see them both soon.”

“Drugs?” Confusion coursed through me at her statement about Aiden.

“Oh yes, apparently Anne used the promise of a weekend away together as a ruse to get him to take care of some extensive dental work he’s been putting off, but he’s a big baby so they had to drug him up really well. I could hear him singing some sort of slurred sonnet to her through the phone.”

Tracy laughed, and I allowed myself to slump down on one of the steps of the staircase. I’d seen flashes of exploding appendixes and hospital rooms at the mention of Aiden on drugs, and it frightened me. The relief I felt at knowing it was just a few sore teeth that had delayed him was immeasurable.

When Tracy finally stopped laughing at herself, she spoke again. “So, come on, Gillie. Guess how much they offered?”

“I don’t know, Tracy. How much?”

“They’ve offered to pay you one hundred thousand dollars for three nights at the castle. And you don’t even have to leave. You, Aiden, the dog, everyone can stay right where you are since there’s plenty of room for everyone.”

It was the first time Tracy had mentioned Toby since she left, and I knew I needed to lay claim on him right away. I glanced down at the young boy to see Toby crawled up in his lap, licking his face while Cooper laughed and stroked the dog affectionately. My heart swelled up with love for the little ball of fluff.

"Tracy, before you explain all of this stuff, I want to talk to you about the dog. I've grown rather fond of him and..." I hesitated and Tracy surprised me by relieving my anxiety before I even had a chance to voice my concern.

"I know. He's yours now, Gillie. That's why I called you. The dog is yours, the castle is yours, the money that the guests coming tonight will leave is yours to give to Aiden so he can finish the renovations. In short, little sister, everything is yours."

Chapter 4

Just Outside Cagair Castle—1649

Dusk set in by the time he reached the top of the cliff leading to Cagair Castle. He found the climb to be easier than ever before—a sure sign that Marion was right and it was time for him to move on, to find something to fill his time until the day he would remember. He had to believe that his memories would return, for the sake of his own sanity if nothing else.

Each time he climbed up the rocks, a sense of familiarity coursed through him, but it was a feeling he didn't understand, a feeling he didn't trust. He knew it had to be some part of him that could still recall his fall but so many things seemed strangely familiar, yet out of reach. He never knew if they were a true memory or if they were only the result of his broken mind playing tricks on him.

He wouldn't enter the village tonight. If he did, he didn't imagine that he would be able to return to Marion, and he wanted to say goodbye before he left her for good. From all he could tell, the island Cagair Castle sat upon and the village near it were isolated from much of Scotland. If he fell from the rocks here, it stood to reason that he'd lived not far from the castle.

In a village so small, if his suspicions were correct, someone would recognize him right away. He wasn't ready for things to change so drastically. Instead, he would wait at the top of the rocks and watch the castle carefully to make sure that no one was about and then move across the grounds so that he could travel over the bridge. From there he planned to make his way around the village and look in from the outside. Perhaps that way, he could plan where to start his inquiries in the morning.

Despite his fears, he knew he had to risk traveling into the village come morning and with that, it was very possible someone would know him and the truth about himself would be revealed. For now he could only hope that he was the sort of man before the fall that he believed himself to be now. If, by chance, no one recognized him in the village come morning, he would look for work.

No one ever seemed to move about Cagair Castle at night, but with the last bit of sunlight still remaining, he knew he should wait awhile just to make sure. He settled in at the top of the rocks, looking up at the castle and across it over to the small set of stables that sat next to a stone house, built assuredly for the stablemaster to live and work. It looked sturdy and small and to him, rather perfect. No candlelight burned from within and, setting aside his better judgment, he decided to venture closer.

He moved quietly, making sure to go around the back, peering in one of two windows as carefully as he could. Finding it empty, he moved over to the stables and stood outside to listen for the sound of someone working. All he could hear were the horses. He found that a sense of hope rose within him. Perhaps he would have to look no further than here for something to sustain him. It seemed a more preferable prospect than venturing down to the village. He hoped he could show the laird the work he was capable of doing for him. If Cagair Castle needed someone to care for the horses, he would gladly take the job.

A job here, far from the village, would buy him the time to try and remember without being thrust back into a life unfamiliar to him. It was the very thing he feared the most about venturing into the village.

He didn't feel the same fear here around the castle. For surely, whatever his life had been before, it hadn't involved living amongst such powerful Scottish landowners—with working and living so close to such a grand castle. No, he imagined that his life had been much simpler than all of that. No one would know him here on the island of Cagair Castle.

He must have dozed outside the stables. When the sound of voices woke him, the moon was the only source of light among the darkness. He stood quickly, stepping backwards so that he couldn't be seen. He leaned forward and strained to listen.

"Did he seriously run through there ahead of us? The child has no fear. It's genuinely a problem. He's traveled through so many times, he doesn't think it's a big deal anymore. I'm about to be sick at the thought of bringing these two babies through. Every time I've gone through, I've felt bad for days after."

The sound of the woman's voice surprised him. It differed so greatly from Marion's form of speech or his own, but he could understand the plain dialect of what the woman said. It made him wonder if, at some point in his life, he'd heard someone speak in much the same way as this woman before.

He stepped away from the stables and moved quietly around the small house, standing beside it so that he could hear them more clearly. He could see the shadows of two women. The one who just spoke balanced a small child on each hip, while the other moved in to comfort her before speaking.

"Grace, this one, for whatever reason, is different. It doesn't seem to hurt anyone at all. It's rather strange, really—it takes coming out of the stairwell for you to realize that the travel worked. Cooper's fine, I'm sure. He's just waiting for us on the other side. You wait here, and I'll go get the guys. Then, we need to go on through."

The second woman stepped away and, in a moment, she appeared at the side of the castle followed by two men. He couldn't make out their features, but he had to push his feet hard into the ground to keep himself from running up to the group of strangers. Something within him wanted to be near all of them, wanted to speak to them and follow them wherever they were so obviously headed. He refrained and watched curiously as they neared an unexpected opening in the side of the castle.

They entered it one by one. While he sat under the moonlight watching, he tried to imagine how large the space could possibly be. Surely it wasn't large enough to hold all of them comfortably, not unless it was a tunnel that traveled under the length of the castle. He decided to approach. Once he stood next to the castle stones, he took his time traveling around its perimeter, looking for any possible place where they could have come out the other side. When he found nothing, he approached the doorway from which they'd all left.

He knew he should walk away, return to Marion, and spend the evening with her before trying to talk to the castle's laird in the morning, but he couldn't bring himself to leave the strange doorway. He stood as still as the stones around him, scarcely breathing so that he might hear any movement beyond the doorway.

Long moments passed before he worked up the nerve to open the doorway. The moonlight shined down into the stairwell. When he gazed within, he couldn't believe what he saw—no tunnel or room lay at the bottom, only a wall of stones. Each person that he watched enter was most assuredly now gone.

Chapter 5

Cagair Castle—Present Day

"I'm sorry. What did you just say?" I pressed the phone hard against my ear so that I could be sure. I didn't want to misunderstand a word that she said.

She repeated the same sentiment.

"You heard me, Gillie. It was foolish of me to buy the place. I know that. I knew it the day I signed the papers. My first thought was to give it to you, but then I started thinking about all of the work that still needed to be done, and I knew that Mark would never let me pay for it if there was no chance at a return. Anyway, then I received this phone call from a woman who offered to rent the castle for such a ridiculous amount of money. I couldn't say no.

"That was three days ago, and I've been arranging everything ever since. I'm sorry I didn't tell you sooner. I know that the guests will be arriving this evening, but I've no doubt that you'll handle that just fine."

My head spun and ached as I tried to process everything she said. I wanted to smile and jump and dance around the room for joy that I wouldn't have to leave this place, but I wanted to be certain before I allowed myself to feel anything other than skepticism.

I had to scream her name into the phone to get her to stop talking. "Tracy. You have to slow down. You're throwing a lot at me, and I'm having a hard time keeping up."

I listened to her take a deep breath and a slight pause before she spoke again. This time, her voice was much lower, slower, and she enunciated every word.

"I've been hurrying because I'm about to miss our plane. We're headed to Italy for a few weeks, and I'm afraid I'll be out of contact. Listen to me carefully, Gillian. I'm giving you the house, okay? And the dog. I'm pretty sure he wouldn't come with me even if I wanted him to at this point, so he's yours as well. I can't use our money to restore the place anymore if it's in your name, but you can use the money from the guests to do that."

"Tracy." My hands were shaking with the surge of excitement and disbelief that surged through me. "That's really too much."

"It's already done, Gillie. Look, I have to go, but I'm sending a lawyer over with the paperwork a week from today, after the guests have gone. He can answer any questions you may have."

The light click followed by silence was the only indication that our conversation was over. As I slipped the phone back in my pocket, I had to grip the handrail to pull myself up on the stairs.

In one brief moment, everything that I dreamed about this place from the moment I came to stay here was a reality. I would have to write Tracy one hell of a thank-you note after everything was finished here—not that there would be any real address to send it to.

Laughter traveled up the stairwell, and I suddenly remembered the little boy in the foyer. I looked down to see him giggling while Toby bounced around him like a rabbit. I walked down the stairs toward him just as Aiden appeared in the doorway with Anne at his side. She had a firm grip on his arm, and I could tell she did her best to steer him. His eyes were a bit glazed over, his smile a bit too happy, and I couldn't have been more pleased to see him.

"How are you feeling?" I picked up my pace and moved in to give Anne a quick kiss on the cheek first before throwing my arms around Aiden in greeting. Anne released her grip from him for a moment before he swayed slightly on his feet, and we both reached out a hand to steady him.

He surprised me by reaching for my free hand, wrapping his fingers around it as he brought it up to his lips and kissed my knuckles gently. I pulled in my brows and looked over at Anne uncomfortably. She burst into laughter.

"Oh, don't mind him. He's been doing that to people all day. He did it to the nurse, and I think she visibly swooned. It's the drugs. They gave him the gas button—can you believe that? And, as you can see, he got a little bit carried away with it. Not to mention that he's already popped one of his pain pills. The combination has him rather loopy. At least he's a happy drunk."

I laughed and pulled my hand away from him. "Yes, clearly."

Anne and I moved him inside the entryway as Anne looked around the room curiously before turning to address Cooper.

"Well, hello there. Are you the only guest? Where are your parents? Tracy made it sound like there would be a bunch of you."

The boy stood and dusted off his shorts before walking over to her.

"Oh, there are. They're just coming along behind me. I needed to stretch my legs, so they let me out before the bridge so I could run the rest of the way."

This version differed from what he'd told me before, and alarm bells went off in my head.

"Wait a minute. You told me earlier the cars dropped you all off before the bridge and you just ran ahead of them. Just now, you said they let you out of the car so you could run ahead. Which is it? Either way, they should be here by now, shouldn't they?"

I watched as the child's face reddened, and I knew he didn't know how to dig himself out of the lie though I couldn't imagine why he felt the need to lie in the first place. Their stay had already been arranged.

I waited, saying nothing to give the boy an opportunity to decide how he wanted to proceed. He opened and closed his mouth a dozen times before a ruckus of noise outside saved him.

"That's them. They're here."

He ran out the front door to greet the rest of his family. Once he was gone, Anne turned to me suspiciously.

"I just drove down the bridge. There was no car, and I didn't see anyone walking."

I shrugged, deciding that in the end, it didn't really matter. Children often told stories, I assumed, and it wasn't really my place to reprimand him. I would ask one of the adults after everyone made it inside.

Cooper was the first to re-enter, his hand clasping that of a beautiful little girl, just barely with her footing underneath her as she wobbled along behind whom I assumed was her brother. Next came a beautiful blonde who had her hands full with another small baby. She smiled at me as she entered, but she looked stressed and weary. She had every right to be after traveling with so many little ones.

Then came two of the tallest, fittest, most gorgeous men I'd ever seen in my life, and I found myself swallowing just to keep my mouth from falling open. I glanced over at Anne and smiled with satisfaction at seeing her eyes bug out of her head. It pleased me to know that I wasn't the only one affected by their appearance.

Both men nodded politely as they stepped inside. I thought for a moment that they were about to say something when another blonde—equally as beautiful as the first—walked in and immediately made her way over to us, extending her hand in my direction.

"Hi, you must be…is it Gillian? Your sister referred to you as Gillie, but I wouldn't want to call you that if it's a family name."

I smiled, shook her hand, and decided that I liked her very much right away. She was personable, confident, and friendly—not at all like the stuck-up, rich group of snobs I expected when Tracy first mentioned the dollar amount they would be paying.

"It's not a family name really. Tracy is the only one who calls me that so yes, please call me Gillian."

"Great. I'm Jane." She released my hand and took a step back to glance around the room.

"Isn't it wonderful, Aunt Jane? It's looks so much the same, only without so many candles, and it's not as cold." It was Cooper's voice that spoke. Only then did I notice that Jane's eyes had filled with tears once she stepped away.

"Yes, Coop. It's amazing." Jane stepped back until she stood next to one of the men. She reached out to take his hand in comfort.

I could tell Cagair Castle meant a great deal to at least part of the group, and suddenly it made so much more sense as to why they'd come—some of them had been here before. I spoke up, hesitantly.

"Do you like the renovations? We've tried to restore things as accurately as we could, only we've updated a lot of things, made it more functional for modern lives."

The man holding onto Jane's hand spoke, and I noticed the strain in his voice. Seeing the castle moved him as well. "Ye've done a bonny job." He shook his head in near disbelief. "I truly canna tell ye how well ye've done."

I looked over at Anne who seemed to be taking it all in with fascination while she kept a firm grip on Aiden. He looked like he saw dancing purple dinosaurs above their heads.

"Well, it wasn't me." I gestured toward Aiden. "This one deserves all the credit, though I wouldn't attempt to talk to him about it tonight. He's a bit out of it."

The other man, who remained quiet until now, spoke up. "Has he had too much ale then? Do ye need us to help him to bed?"

"No. Not ale. Just laughing gas. I think he can walk okay."

Anne spoke up. "Oh, he can. And I think I'm going to put him to bed right now." She reached out and touched my hand. "I'll let you see them settled, and I'll come back down to talk to you."

As she walked away with Aiden, I returned my attention to Jane. "You've been here before, I guess? How long ago was that?"

Cooper snorted and chuckled briefly before every person in line beside him shot him a look that shut him up right quick. It seemed odd but I'd reached my quota of curious things for the day so I let it pass without question.

"Oh, it's been a good while now. Speaking of people being out of it though, I think we're all pretty worn out from the journey. Would it be okay if we called it a night and we all talked more in the morning? Made proper introductions then?"

"Of course." The day, with its unexpected turns, had worn me out as well. "There are plenty of rooms over on the left side of the staircase, just pick and choose them as you please. The right side is ours."

Jane nodded. Before I could say another word, everyone save her took off in that direction with no hesitation whatsoever. Once they were gone, she turned to speak to me once more.

"I just want to say thank you for letting us impose on you. It's been rather last minute for us as well, but I'll explain that to you tomorrow. Would you like me to give you the check now or when we leave?"

"Oh, when you leave is fine. Jane, can I ask you something?" Try as I might, I couldn't shake the oddity of their unexplained arrival.

"Absolutely."

"How did you all get here? There's no car for you outside."

"We had two cars drop us off, but before we came to the front door, we took a stroll around the grounds. Everyone except Cooper, that is. He decided to walk right up and ring the bell, as you well know."

Her explanation made much more sense than Cooper's, and I couldn't imagine why the young boy hadn't just told me that. Not that it mattered. Her explanation eased any misgivings I had about the situation.

"Ah, that explains a lot then. Okay, you guys have a great night. My room is the third from the right on the top floor. Let me know if you need anything."

She nodded and smiled as she walked away. "Okay, thanks so much."

Jane took two steps before she turned and stared at me for a long minute. It took me speaking to pull her out of it.

"Are you okay? Do you need something?"

When she spoke her voice cracked, and I noticed that her eyes were misty once again.

"Oh, it's nothing. You remind me of a very special memory, is all. I once knew someone who would have liked you very much."

She turned and left me standing in the foyer and, only once I could no longer hear the sound of her footsteps, did Anne, who I'd seen approach from the corner of my eye earlier, dare to speak.

"Well, that was weird."

I nodded. "You heard that, then?"

"Uh, yeah, I did. Their reaction to this place—it's not like one that someone would have if they'd just visited here. It's almost like they lived here or something, yet we know that can't be true. The last owners disappeared and, before them, it sat untouched for years."

"I know. The whole thing is weird." And it was. I half expected to wake up in the morning passed out on the floor of the tower from breathing in too many paint fumes or something.

"You know what else, Gillian? I don't want to freak out but I also heard her say that they walked around the grounds before coming to the front door."

Her words made me nervous. "Yes, what about it?"

"Well, I know he's sort of high, but Aiden just went on and on about it when I tried to put him to bed. He's convinced he saw them crawl out of some cellar in the side of the castle when we pulled up."

My first reaction was to laugh, but Anne's face remained serious.

"That's impossible, Anne. There's not a cellar there."

"I know. Unless we just didn't know about it."

Chapter 6

If such a cellar existed, it was hidden remarkably well. The idea of such a surprise remaining amongst the grounds of the castle during all of the intense construction work kept me awake for most of the night. Finally, when I could take no more of the tossing and turning and wondering, I got myself out of bed around four in the morning, dressed warmly, and made my way outside to look for myself.

I spent over an hour moving slowly around the castle and found nothing. Satisfied that the idea came from Aiden's dental drugs and nothing more, I slipped back inside around five and went down to the modernized kitchen to brew myself a large cup of coffee.

I knew I wouldn't be able to go back to sleep if I went back to bed so, instead, I figured I would jack myself up on caffeine and then go up to the tower to paint. When I started to approach the kitchen, the smell of coffee reached me—someone had already beaten me to the punch.

I expected to find Cooper's mother inside, perhaps rocking a baby or just seeking a few minutes of solitude. When I walked in and saw Cooper himself sitting on the counter right next to the coffee pot, it surprised me to realize that for some reason, I wasn't surprised at all.

"Please tell me you're not drinking that yourself. You're far too young to be hooked on that already."

The young boy smiled and motioned for me to approach him as he extended a mug in my direction.

"This stuff? No way. It tastes like dirt. Aunt Jane really likes it though, so I thought I'd make her some since I was up so early."

"You know how to work the coffee maker?" He couldn't be more than six. I didn't learn how to brew a decent cup until I was in college. I sipped the liquid cautiously. To my surprise, it was delicious.

"Yeah, when I was real little, maybe four, I would stay at my Aunt Jane's a lot, and I always wake up early, you see. It's sort of my thing or something." He smiled and threw his hands up. "I don't know what that means really, but she told me it was my thing. Anyhow, we made a deal because she got tired of me waking her up, and she said that she wouldn't get mad as long as every time I did it, I had a nice big cup of coffee for her to drink. So she showed me. I catch on to things pretty fast."

I smiled and took another gulp. "Oh, I can see that."

Satisfied at his success, Cooper placed the coffee pot back on the warmer and slid off the counter to come and join me at the table. He watched me as I drank. Finally, once he saw that I was nearly done, he spoke.

"Do you have something that you need to do right after this?"

"Not at all." Painting could wait. Even if he did tell tales every now and then, I found the young boy intriguing. "Do you need something?"

"Well, I was just wondering if you might take me on a tour around the castle and show me what you've been doing to everything? I was going to just go on my own, but Mom was pretty mad after I ran ahead of them yesterday. She told me not to go poking around anywhere because this wasn't our house, and it wasn't my place. Since she was already mad, I thought it best to listen."

I laughed and drained the last of my coffee. "Smart man. Sure, I'd love to show you around. Are you ready?"

"Absolutely. Let me just run and get my house shoes. My feet are a little cold."

While he ran off to get something warmer for his feet, I moved over to the cabinet to get a pair of flashlights. All of the electricity was installed, but I didn't want to go turning on all of the lights with everybody still sleeping. By the time I turned around with flashlights in hand, the boy was already at my side. I found it more than a little eerie, how well he seemed to know his way around the castle.

"Okay, do you want to lead the way, or should I?"

He looked at me like I'd asked him a trick question and, in a way, I had. I wanted to see if he would take charge. If he did, I planned to press him further about their history with the place. He was whip smart though, and instead held out a hand in front of him as he turned on his flashlight and illuminated a path for me.

"Me? This isn't my castle. Why don't you go ahead? I'll follow you."

With so many people staying in the castle at the present moment, we found that there were a good many rooms that we couldn't wander into during this time of morning. Still, Cooper seemed to enjoy the parts of the castle that we did see and, even when I went into explaining the exact work that we'd done—conversation that should've been way over his head—he paid attention.

Our last stop was the tower. Since it was separated from most of the other rooms, I didn't hesitate to light up the stairwell leading to it with the modern lighting. As soon as I flipped the switch, Cooper spoke.

"Oh man, that sure helps a lot. I wonder if that had been here the last time I was here, if Isobel would've fallen."

"Who's Isobel?"

Cooper smiled and surprised me by reaching for my hand as we started to walk up the stairs. I didn't know if he offered it for my own benefit or his, but I took it without question.

"Oh, she's a good friend, and she's sort of my boss."

"Your boss? You have a job?"

"Not a real job. I don't get paid money. It's sort of a work for sweets situation. I go each day, even when my Aunt Jane is away with Adwen. Ever since I turned six, my parents started letting me ride alone as long as they watch me until I get there. Anyway, I go every day for just a few hours and help her with some chores and, before I leave, she always gives me something sweet."

I laughed and let loose of his hand when we reached the top landing, speaking to him as I walked to turn on the light in the tower. "Well that sounds like a pretty good deal to me. Do you ever…"

I stopped mid-sentence when I turned to see the way he looked at the painting sitting in the middle of the room—still on its easel, freshly painted and perfect. The child turned white as a ghost, and his lower lip trembled as he looked at it and backed himself up against the wall.

He didn't look frightened, only shocked and confused. When he finally managed the strength to speak, his voice was shaky and breathless as he lifted one little finger to point at my stranger.

"Who is that?"

I watched him carefully. He looked so shaken. I didn't want to upset him by anything I said. Before answering, I approached him slowly. When I stood next to him, I bent to lower myself to his level.

"The man in the painting? I don't know who he is."

Cooper waited and finally he pulled his gaze away from the painting as he turned to face me. His eyes were brimming with tears that were about to fall, and I found myself reaching for him as I pulled him in close.

"Cooper, what's the matter? Do you want me to take it down? I can cover it with something if it will make you feel better. Is it frightening to you?"

"No."

There was a panic in his voice as he answered, a certainty that told me the last thing he wanted me to do was cover it.

"No, don't take it away. I love it. It just…it just surprised me real bad is all."

He lifted himself off my shoulder but kept hold of my hand with one of his own while he reached into one of his pockets with the other.

"I can see that. Why did it surprise you? Do you know who this is?"

He nodded and held out a small, smooth wooden chip. I took it and looked down in astonishment.

It was my stranger, the man I'd painted, carved with remarkable detail into the wood.

"Yes. I know who it is. It's Orick."

So many months of wondering who the man was that came to me in my dreams every single night and now, the child standing next to me knew exactly who he was.

I looked down at my arm. Every hair stood on its end. Chills coursed through my body.

"Who is Orick?"

"He was my buddy, my friend, and so many people loved him very much."

I didn't doubt it. The kindness in his eyes haunted me every moment I was asleep. Whatever woman belonged to him was remarkable lucky.

"If you love him so much, why does the painting upset you?"

Cooper looked me right in the eye as he pulled at my hand.

"It doesn't, it just makes me sad. Why did you paint him? How did you know what he looked like?"

How could I explain what I'd seen night after night when I couldn't explain it to myself? The child would think I was absolutely out of my mind, but I couldn't bring myself to tell him anything but the truth.

"I don't know exactly. Since I've been here, I've seen this man a lot in my dreams, so I decided to paint him—to make him real. But now, hearing you, it seems that I didn't have to do that because he is already real, isn't he?"

"He was real and he was a good, good man, just like my dad and Bebop and E-o and Adwen. But, he's gone now."

I asked the question before his words clicked inside my brain. "What do you mean he's gone?"

Cooper's lip trembled and his tears fell freely as his voice trembled.

"He's dead."

Chapter 7

Marion's Cave—1649

He should have known better than to tell Marion what he'd seen. She was a recluse who lived her life away from all people because of a mistrust of them so deep that he couldn't imagine what happened to make her that way. Of course, she wouldn't be filled with the same sense of wonder and curiosity that he was at what he'd witnessed.

"Doona go near it. 'Tis my advice for ye. No that I expect ye to listen to a word that I say. 'Twill only cause ye heartache if ye do. 'Tis the way of such unnatural things."

He crossed his arms and leaned against the side of the cave, hanging onto his patience as best he could.

"Yer guidance means much to me, Marion, whether I choose to listen to it or no. Tell me why. Why should I no follow after the others? Why is heartache the only end?"

Marion exhaled in the same frustrated manner she always did when he disagreed with her.

"Ye just told me that ye watched them walk down the stairs, and they did no come up through the other side, nor did they come out where they went in. Just where do ye think such a staircase could lead when ye saw for yerself that no room lay at the bottom? 'Tis a witch's den. She's already picked the meat from their bones and added them to her stew."

He laughed so loudly that the sound echoed from the walls. Marion glared at him angrily.

"Marion, doona tell such tales, they'll frighten ye when I'm no longer here with ye. They walked into the stairwell with purpose. They knew where it would take them. I know that ye think it no wise, but I…I canna describe it."

He paused and paced around the cave, remembering how his feet had nearly moved toward them against his will.

"'Twas like they called me toward them. In that moment when I saw them, I wanted nothing more than to run and join them, to follow them wherever they might be headed. I canna describe it, but I feel pulled to them, like perhaps they have the answers I seek."

For the first time that evening, Marion stopped twiddling away at the piece of wood she held in her hands and stopped to regard him seriously.

"Do ye mean it? Ye felt so strongly about the people ye saw there? Do ye think mayhap ye would have felt the same with whomever ye saw first after leaving here?"

He shrugged. He asked himself the same thing on his way back to the cave the night before, but the more he allowed the question to linger, the more his mind rebelled against it. The truth was making its way to the surface of his mind. He could feel it building within him. He just couldn't grasp at it alone. All he needed was to find the keys to unlock it, the people to remind him of the memories he lost.

The strange-speaking women and the men that accompanied them pulled at something inside him that made him wonder if they were those very keys.

"I canna know, but I doona think so. I felt as if I knew them, but I couldna recall any real memory of them. I just know that I feel strongly that the stairwell is where I must start."

He moved across the small expanse of the cave and sat down next to Marion. Her gaze softened as he did so.

They sat quietly next to one another for a long time until, finally, Marion spoke.

"Then start there, ye must, whether it be a witch's den or no. 'Tis time, Craig. Time for the two of us to part ways."

He stood with a sadness in his heart he couldn't deny. All of his memories were of Marion—there was nothing else inside his mind. He wondered often if he meant as much to her as she did to him, if she would grieve for the end of their friendship as he would. She spoke little about her feelings, but he knew that didn't mean she was void of them.

"I will miss ye, Marion. If I pass this way again, should I come to see ye?"

"No."

The abruptness of her answer pained him.

"I willna be here. This cave was no my first home, nor will it be my last. I move often and 'tis time that I move on. I was on my way elsewhere when I saw ye fall."

All of that was new to him. Foolishly, he imagined Marion spending a great many years in the cave, and now he learned that she may have only been here a fortnight when he arrived.

He would feel lost once he left her—without her, every person in the world would be a stranger to him.

"Marion, ye canna know how grateful I am to ye. I wish I could repay ye for all ye've done for me."

She shook her head and moved to stand at the entrance of the cave as if waiting for him to leave. Her shortness bothered him. That she could say so little in their last moment together. He said nothing, only made his way past her, stopping to lean in and kiss her cheek before stepping away and out of the cave.

For the first few steps, he thought she would allow him to leave without another word but eventually, she called out to him. He turned to look at his friend one last time.

There were tears in her eyes, a sight he'd never seen before. He moved in to comfort her, but she held a hand up to stop him.

"Ye must go, Craig. If ever ye find a group of people who care for ye more than I, doona ye dare leave them, for ye will be a lucky man."

Chapter 8

Present Day

Cooper's revelation freaked me out enough that I spent the rest of the day in the solitude of my bedroom wondering if Aiden was right. Could Cagair Castle really be haunted? But did ghosts usually visit people in their dreams? I didn't know, having no experience with anything paranormal myself. Regardless, the idea that I'd been daydreaming, night-dreaming, painting, and fantasizing about a dead man gave me the heebie-jeebies worse than walking in on my aunt and uncle getting busy in my grandparents' lake house.

And the thing was, no one else had seen this man around the castle. Not the construction workers, or Aiden, or Anne. So what did that say about me? Was I crazy, or was it not so much the castle that was haunted but just me? The entire thing was unsettling and, really, rather embarrassing. I'd spent hours upon hours reading nonsense into my dreams—hoping, wondering if perhaps I was somehow meant to know this man—that maybe in another life, or just later in this one, I might love him. Any chance of that happening was clearly now shot to hell.

I spent a miserable night trying to stay awake and then, in the end, fell asleep only to have the same beautiful dead man hanging out behind my eyelids. Come morning, exhausted and rather peeved, I went to check in on Aiden to see if he needed anything now that Anne had left for the day to go and check on things back at their real home.

I found him already awake, dressed, and sitting at the end of his bed slipping on shoes as if he were about to head to work. That so wasn't going to happen today. If I allowed it, I would never hear the end of it from Anne.

"How are you feeling? Whatever you say, I know it's not well enough to be slipping on your work boots."

He stilled his hands on the laces of his shoes and lifted himself so that he could cross his arms and stare back at me.

"My wife just left. I can do without ye bossing me around, as well. I feel fine, a bit sore but better than yesterday."

Yesterday, after the copious amount of drugs he took the day of surgery, had been miserable for the poor guy. Anne restricted the pain pills, and he'd not felt like doing anything but lying around and having her baby him.

"Well, I'm glad you're feeling a little better, but I don't think you need to do any work today. The construction crew can't come back until after everybody leaves so just take it easy for a while, yeah? Think of it as a little vacation."

He could see that he fought a losing battle and kicked his shoes off with a frown.

"I doona want another 'vacation.' The last dinna go well."

I grinned and stepped inside the room, moving to sit on a small bench opposite him.

"Yeah, it was awful mean what she did to you. Though, I'm sure she'll make it up to you somehow."

Aiden lifted his eyebrows mischievously. "Aye, I'll make sure she does. What are ye doing here, Gillian? I expected ye'd already have half a canvas painted by now."

"I'm going to take a break from painting during the day for a while. Let our guests have their run of the place. I'm just trying to stay out of their way. They all seem very preoccupied preparing for whoever they are hosting here tonight." I paused and bit my lip as I tried to approach the strange subject with Aiden. Eventually, I decided to just go for it. "Hey, you want to hear something really creepy?"

He smiled with wide eyes. "Aye, always."

"Okay, so you know that painting you commented on the other day? The one of the man?"

"Mr. Needs-To-Eat-More-Cookies-And-Less-Protein-Shakes? Aye, I remember the painting. What about it?"

I laughed at Aiden's description of him. The same thought had crossed my mind more than a few times—the man's body fat had to be like some sort of ridiculous negative percentage.

"Well, I've been dreaming about him, you know? And, yesterday morning, I bumped into the small kid that's here—Cooper? You probably don't remember his name since you were high as a kite when they got here but anyway, he wanted me to show him around the castle, so I did, and…" I hesitated, chills scattering over my arms just thinking back on it. "When he saw the painting, he looked like he'd seen a ghost."

Aiden's brows pulled in and his smile faded. "Why would he do that?"

"He knew the man in the painting. He knew him very well. That man is dead now."

"Aye, ye were no joking when ye said creepy."

"I know." My voice lifted an octave as I answered him. "I don't know what to think about it. I dreamed about him last night again too."

"Do ye think Cagair was his home? Maybe ye should switch bedrooms?"

I shook my head and stood to move around the room in an effort to calm my nerves. "I don't think that he did, but I don't know. I didn't ask the boy anything more. It seemed to upset him so much. I just sort of dropped it and brought him back downstairs."

"Ask the lad's parents."

I couldn't do that. I already promised Cooper that I wouldn't.

"I can't. He thought the painting would upset his Aunt Jane and Uncle Adwen even more than it did him. He didn't want anyone else to know about it."

Aiden reached up to rub his hand over his face like he always did when he was thinking something over. When he spoke, his tone was entirely serious.

"He's trying to tell ye something, Gillian. Ye've got to listen to him. It's the only way he will leave ye alone."

"But he never says anything. I just see him. I don't know how I could listen to him any more. I dream about him. I've painted him. If he's a ghost, why doesn't he just act like a normal one and stay out of my head and show up in the hallway?"

Aiden stood and walked over to look down the hallway as if he thought my words would summon the man straight from his grave. "Doona say that unless ye mean it. Ye shouldna invite them in. Enough wander this world on their own as it is."

"I do mean it. I'm tired of this and more than a little freaked out by it now that I know this man is dead and not my soul mate."

Aiden laughed, easing the creepy tension that had built quickly.

"Yer soul mate? Why I wouldna have picked ye to be the kind to think of something so fanciful. If he were yer soul mate, he wouldna be dead, and ye'd be far more likely to meet him in an airport rather than yer dreams."

My face warmed in embarrassment. "Yeah, well obviously, I know that now but at first, it seemed logical."

Aiden shook his head in amusement. It made me want to jab him in the cheek with one of my fingers, just to aggravate his sore teeth.

"Logical? Ha. There is nothing logical about ye women folk."

I couldn't argue with him. Now, knowing what I did, it seemed ridiculous.

"Okay, I regret having told you any of that, frankly. Let's just move on from it."

Aiden started to speak but stopped as someone cleared his throat in the doorway. It was Adwen, Jane's husband who I'd been formally introduced to the day before. He looked concerned, and he started talking as soon as we both noticed him.

"I am sorry to interrupt the two of ye, but I'm afraid that I've received some bad news and must leave at once."

I stood and made my way over to him. "I'm so sorry. Is there anything I can do to help?"

"I doona think so, but thank ye for the offer. 'Tis my brother and Da. They travel often and I doona worry, but they dinna arrive where they were meant to over a fortnight ago. My other brother is leaving this evening to go in search of them, and I doona feel that I should leave him to go alone."

"Of course not. Are the others leaving as well?" Two weeks seemed like a very long time for people to be missing and there just now to be concern over it, but evidently news traveled a little more slowly amongst Cagair Castle's newest guests.

"No, this is too important to Jane and Grace, and I'm sure no harm has come to them. I wager they just changed their minds about where they were headed and either dinna send word to those expecting them or they sent a man to give word of their new direction and he dinna do as he was asked."

I couldn't bring myself to bite my tongue. "Why wouldn't they just call those who were expecting and tell them themselves?"

The corner of Adwen's mouth turned up in a peculiar smile, and I could tell then that despite his need to leave and see to them, he truly wasn't all that worried. "They doona have phones with them nor anywhere near where they're traveling."

"Are they traveling in Antarctica?"

Aiden walked over to join us while we were talking and suddenly jabbed me in the ribs as if I'd said something very rude.

Adwen just laughed, ignoring me completely as he turned to talk to Aiden.

"I know that I havena met ye yet, but ye seem a good enough man. Could I ask ye a favor? 'Tis no a small one, and I doona know if yer wife would approve of it."

His question piqued Aiden's curiosity and immediately he gave his permission. "Aye. What do ye need?"

I stepped back and watched the two of them as Adwen shifted uncomfortably between his feet. I couldn't wait to hear what he said.

"We are here because Jane and Grace received word that their parents were coming from America for a visit. They dinna ask if they could come, only told them when and where they would meet them. The lassies are no that close with them, but I guess their parents have decided that long enough has passed since they've seen them. They've never met me nor Eoghanan, and while Jane understands why I must go, she worries that they will think she made me up if I am no there."

The oddities of these people seemed to grow by the second. They'd rented a castle for an obscene amount of money, Aiden was convinced they'd arrived here by crawling out of some sort of cellar that didn't exist, they knew the man who was haunting me in my sleep, and now, it almost sounded like Adwen meant to suggest that Aiden step in and take his place.

Aiden must have come to the same conclusion for his entire face pinched up uncomfortably in confusion. "I'm sorry, I doona understand what I can do to help with that."

"I'm asking that ye pretend to be me for the evening. Jane is fine with it, and the others willna give way to the truth."

I almost refrained from speaking up, but if he didn't want me to hear anything, he should've asked when I wasn't around. "I'm sorry but how will that ever work? Even if they believe it now, it's not like Aiden will be around every time you see your in-laws. That's sort of a ridiculous thing to ask him."

"'Tis the only occasion I'll have to see my in-laws for some time and, from what I've heard about them, they both keep themselves in a state no unlike the one Aiden was in the night we arrived."

Aiden looked like he'd just been asked to save the world. His face lit up with excitement, and he lifted his chest like he was ready to start the charade right away.

"Hush, Gillian, and mind yer own business. If that's true, then I'll have no problem doing as ye've asked. As far as my wife goes, she willna mind. If I know her at all, she'll enjoy watching the spectacle. I'm in."

Chapter 9

"Gillian, just what exactly are you looking for? You look sort of crazy, and I'm worried that you might fall out of the window if you lean any farther out."

Grunting, I clicked off the flashlight and pulled myself back inside before closing the window and twisting to look at Anne. She wore sweats and had her hair pulled up casually and had a frozen pizza she'd just warmed in one hand and a bottle of wine in the other. She was all prepared for our grown-up sleepover. We planned to eat way too much food, drink way too much wine, eavesdrop on Aiden's charade as much as we could and, despite my profound objections, summon the ghost of Orick using some sort of scary-ass book Anne picked up in Glasgow.

"I feel crazy, Anne. I really, really do, but I'm telling you, I just can't shake the feeling that something is way off with these people. I think Aiden was right about them that first night here. It doesn't make sense that they don't have a car, and what sort of car service do you know of that brings people all the way out here?"

Anne glared at me and shut the bedroom door as she set down the wine and pizza. "I don't know of any, truthfully, but that doesn't mean one doesn't exist. Have you gotten into Aiden's pain pills or something because you're starting to sound a lot like him? If you have, I'm not letting you into this wine. I can't handle that sort of crazy tonight."

"No." I walked across the room and grabbed the corkscrew off the table, working away at the wine bottle while I spoke. "I have not been into the pain pills." The cork popped out of the bottle, and I paused to take it off of the corkscrew before pouring us each a hearty glass. "You know how Adwen had to leave? Well, I started questioning him about a car, and he kept insisting that he would walk down into the village where someone would pick him up."

Anne swallowed a big swig before shrugging her shoulders at me, annoyed. "So?"

"So?" I sat my glass down so I could swing my arms about in aggravation. "So? Who does that? Who walks all the way into the village in the mist and the rain?"

"People who like walking."

I shook my head, frustrated that she didn't see the oddity in his behavior. "I like walking, but not in the rain. It was just too weird so I insisted that he let me drive him and guess what? The whole way there he acted just as stressed as he could be—like he didn't really need to go to the village at all."

Anne laughed and moved to fill up her glass.

"Please don't tell me that you're suggesting he didn't need to go into the village because he actually needed to walk around to the side of the castle and leave through some secret cellar."

I looked down at my glass as I answered her. "That's exactly what I'm suggesting."

"Oh, come on, Gillian. You looked already. I looked too and didn't find anything. Aiden just made that up or dreamed it or something. You remember how out of it he was that night."

"I do remember, but you can't deny how weird these people are."

For the first time, she nodded in agreement. "They are weird and the whole thing with the painting is super bizarre, but so what? They're paying you a ton of money to be here, and they will leave the day after tomorrow so just suck it up and don't worry about it right now."

I placed both hands over my face and exhaled as calmly as I could.

"Fine."

"Great. Now, why don't you tell me just exactly what you were doing hanging out the window when I walked in here?"

"Oh." I glanced over at the still open window and the flashlight lying on the end of my bed. "I was watching for Adwen, trying to see if he would walk back over here from the village."

Anne didn't say anything, only shook her head and sat down her glass of wine before moving to open the door and step out into the hallway.

I stood and followed her out of the room. "What are you doing?"

"I'm not going to do anything other than stand there and watch, but you need to go downstairs and give a quick welcome to Jane and Grace's parents so we can get back up here and eat our pizza."

"What?" I backed back into the room. "I don't need to do that."

She smiled and gave a funny little giggle that made me wonder if she'd started in on the wine a little before coming to my room.

"You're right, but it will give us a chance to see how Aiden's faring. I'm very curious."

The moment we walked into the small sitting room that lay off the grand dining hall, I knew it was a mistake. The group was deep in a heated conversation about Cooper, and they all hushed immediately when the old man spotted Anne and me lingering in the doorway.

Sweat hung visibly on Aiden's brow, and I could tell he already regretted his agreement.

"Can we help you with something?"

It was the old man who spoke and, immediately, I didn't like him. His glare, his tone, his posture—everything about the way he carried himself screamed that he believed himself to be above me, and he didn't appreciate my intrusion.

"I just wanted to welcome you to Cagair Castle. I hope you have a lovely visit with your daughters. Please don't hesitate to let me know if you need anything."

The man turned away from me, not bothering to thank me or address me further as he spoke to his daughters as if I weren't there.

"Why would your contractor feel the need to come and welcome us to the castle? In truth, I'm rather surprised to find you've hired a woman. I assumed it was a man."

I started to protest, but Jane stood and spoke up before I had the chance.

"Yes. Yes, she's a she and she's done a wonderful job, don't you think. She came to welcome you because she's polite, Father. Why don't you extend her the same courtesy?"

The old scrooge turned and nodded at me in apology before opening his mouth to start in on Anne.

"And who is that? Surely not someone you've hired. She's dressed so slovenly."

"She's the cook." Jane stared right at us, clearly pleading with her eyes for us to go along with whatever she said.

"The cook? Then, why is she dressed like that?"

"Because *she...*" Anne put great emphasis on the word as she spoke up, making it evident she didn't appreciate being talked about like she wasn't there. Anne always spoke her mind, but I had a feeling that the wine made her even braver than usual. "...is off-duty. Now, if you'll excuse us."

She pulled at my arm as we stepped away from the doorway, and I could hear her seething the entire way as I followed her back up to my bedroom.

Once the door was closed, she let loose on me.

"What an awful, horrible man. Why, I'd like to shove this soon-to-be-empty wine bottle right up his ass—not that there's room since he's so full of shit."

I allowed my eyes to bug out of my head in the shock I felt at her manner of speech before I collapsed into a fit of giggles that nearly brought me down to the floor.

In a short moment, she joined right in along with me, and I knew whatever anger she had before was now gone.

"He was terrible but Jane behaved even more strangely. Do her parents think that she owns this castle? Why else would she say I was the contractor?"

Anne pulled on the chair tucked into the crook of my desk and took a seat as she answered.

"You know, downstairs I didn't know what to think about any of it, but you must be right. Okay, I think I'm on board with you now. The whole thing is creepy—you deserve far more explanation than they've given you, no matter how much they are willing to pay."

I raised my glass to hers so that we could clink them together. "Agreed. I'll talk to Jane about it in the morning but, tonight, let's just enjoy some girl time."

Anne pointed to the old book she had laid open on the table with a smile that sent dread running through me.

"And let's summon the spirit of that gorgeous dead man who keeps haunting you."

"I'm going to need more wine before I have the courage to get started in any of that business. Would you mind going over to close the window, Anne? The rain seems to be blowing a bit horizontally."

Wine glass in hand, Anne moved over to the window, leaning out of it to breathe in the wet air.

"It smells so lovely, and the wind actually feels kind of nice. Do you want to go run around in it?"

I snickered from across the room. "You're quite the lightweight aren't you, Anne?"

She didn't answer me, and I assumed she couldn't hear me with the way she had her head hanging out the window as she tossed her head back and forth trying to catch raindrops with her tongue.

I turned away from her to grab a slice of pizza just as she let out a horrified shriek.

"What is it?"

I ran over to her as she pulled herself back inside, wide eyes and shock on her face.

"There's a man out there, Gillian."

"A man." Instantly I thought of Adwen and anger surged through me. I moved over to the bed to grab my flashlight. "I knew it. I knew that lying rat didn't need to go to the village."

Anne shut the window and ran over to follow me as I walked toward the door.

"It didn't look like Adwen."

"It's dark outside, Anne. How could you tell?"

"I know it's dark but I'm telling you, I don't think it was Adwen. Maybe it was the ghost—maybe we summoned him."

I shook my head and brushed past her. "It's not the ghost. We haven't even started to try and summon him yet. Are you coming with me or are you staying here?"

Anne shook her head so hard that water droplets from the rain scattered around the room.

"No way. I'm staying here. If it's Adwen, I think it's best that you have that confrontation on your own and just tell me about it later, and if it's the ghost…well, I don't think I can take that. So, you're on your own."

"That's fine. Just save me some pizza. I'll be back with that lying creep in tow in just a few minutes."

I left her and marched down the castle's back set of steps as my frustration grew with each step downward. I would go out the back doorway, so as not to impose on the other group of liars in the front of the castle.

The wind blew so fiercely that I had to pull the door with all of my might to get it to open. When it finally did, I fell backward a few steps, catching myself on the wall as I looked up to see a tall shadow standing in the doorway.

Every ounce of breath left my body in one fell swoop as shock and fear paralyzed me.

Anne was right. Adwen wasn't heading toward the imaginary cellar.

My ghost stood not two feet from me.

Chapter 10

The lass looked terrified but, even as the color drained from her cheeks, he knew she was the very reason he felt pulled to walk down the secret set of steps. He didn't know her, not her name or why she dressed so differently from Marion, but he'd seen those fiery locks of hair before.

Even without the memory in his mind, he knew she was why he was here. It was an overwhelming connection he couldn't explain. Whether it was from a memory lost to him or it was still to come, he knew the lass standing before him would hold his heart.

He wanted to reach for her, to pull her against him and into an embrace so that his fingers could wind their way up into her locks of hair. Perhaps she was the witch whose den Marion suspected he would wander into, for with eyes so green, he felt she bewitched his very soul.

He still didn't understand what happened to him in the stairwell. He walked down the steps but, instead of finding a tunnel or a room, he was swallowed by a watery wall he couldn't make sense of. He thought it killed him for sleep found him quickly—a dark, strange sleep that seemed like it would go on forever until he woke inside the same stairwell as before.

Eager to avoid the same unconsciousness once more, he fled the steps, crawling back out onto the lawn as if nothing had happened. Confused and eager to find shelter from the rain, he looked for the nearest door of the castle. Just as he neared it, the door flung itself open to reveal the woman he stared back at now.

"I'm sorry, lass. I dinna mean to frighten ye. 'Twas the door nearest me. I only meant to escape the storm."

He watched her as she opened and closed her mouth as if the words she wanted to say wouldn't come, and he wondered for a moment if she were mute.

Slowly, so as not to frighten her, he took a step closer. The lass had fallen backwards from the weight of the door but caught herself with the wall, and she still held herself up against it. He extended his hand toward her, hoping to help pull her upright. The movement startled her, and he stepped back into the rain at the shock of hearing her voice.

"No, no, no. You just stay back. Are you…I'm going to touch you, okay?"

Her words surprised him both in meaning and in tone. She was breathless, shaking all over, but still her eyes held a curiosity and fearlessness that he admired. He nodded his permission and closed his eyes as her hand reached toward him. She gently placed her palm on his chest, her fingers resting on the side of his neck.

It took his breath away and tightened the muscles of his stomach as he forced his eyes to open as she spoke.

"Holy mother of God. You are not a ghost, are you? You're not dead."

He stepped toward her again so that he stood underneath the overhang and out of the rain as he leaned into the doorway.

"No, lass. I am verra pleased to tell ye that I am no a ghost, and I am no dead yet. I must ask ye though, do ye know me? Did ye think I was dead?"

He had to remind himself to breathe as he waited for her answer. He desperately wanted to hear her say *yes*. He wanted her to know him in the way he wanted to know her. If she was the life he'd forgotten, he could walk into the future unafraid whether he remembered or not.

"If I did know you, wouldn't you know who I was?"

His heart sank at her answer.

"No, I'm afraid that I wouldna. I took a fall many moons ago, and I canna remember anything before that. I was saved by a cave dwelling lass and just this eve have left her company to go in search of who I was."

He didn't know enough about people to read the girl's expression, but she looked more shocked to him now than she did when she first laid eyes on him.

"Are you serious, or are you just another part of the crazy that has invaded Cagair Castle over the last few days?"

He didn't know what she was talking about.

"Aye, I'm verra serious. No, I doona believe that I am."

The woman's eyes softened toward him. Slowly, she waved him inside.

"Okay, then. It must be very hard for you to not remember anything."

Once he stepped inside, she reached around him and closed the door, bumping into his chest as she did so. She stilled, and he didn't miss the way her breath caught at the impact. He didn't know if she was frightened or if she felt the same exquisite thump of her heart as he did—he very much hoped it was the latter.

"'Tis verra hard. I live with guilt for those who may have missed me, though I canna see their faces, nor do I know their names. 'Tis as if I love people I've never met. All I want to do is know them again."

She didn't step away from him. He reveled in their closeness, though he made no move to touch her. They simply stood together near the doorway.

"Do you know your own name?"

He looked down at her and, as she looked up at him, the words seemed to leave him. She made him nervous in a way that lit his chest on fire, turned his voice into a whisper, and made his breeches uncomfortable.

"No, lass. I know only what Marion called me, and she called me Craig. Ye may call me that if ye wish it."

She smiled. He felt the warmth of it to his very core.

"No. Your name isn't Craig."

Apparently, he wasn't the only one who thought the name didn't suit him. "Aye, I know that. It never seemed like my name, but she insisted she call me that. I wish I knew what it was, though my name is only one of many things I wish I knew."

The woman's voice when she spoke was but a whisper, but she smiled as she said it.

"I know what your name is. It's Orick. Your name is Orick."

"Just how would ye know that, lass, if ye doona know me?"

The moment he heard her utter the name, he knew it was true. He'd been called the name before. To hear it now, one small piece that felt familiar, took his breath away from him.

He wanted to kiss her for the joy it brought him. He wanted to kiss her for far more than that, but he refrained and looked down into her eyes while he waited for her to answer.

"I don't know you. Not really. Although, I feel like I do. I know some people who know you—some people who will be very happy and quite overwhelmed to see you."

How could he be so lucky? To find what he'd lost in his very first stop after leaving Marion. Happiness, fear, nerves, hope—so many emotions surged through him hearing such news that tears sprung to his eyes unbeknownst to him until the lass reached up to brush one from the corner of his eye.

He stepped back, embarrassed by his show of emotion until she reached out to give his hand a gentle squeeze.

"It's okay. Of course hearing something like that would touch you. Would you like to meet them?"

"Oh, more than ye know, lass."

She smiled at him and stepped away, nudging her head toward the staircase as she started to walk off in front of him.

"Good. You will, but not quite yet. Come with me."

Chapter 11

I should have been frightened by the sight of a man I thought was dead and was just a few mere minutes away from trying to summon up from his grave, but I wasn't. Startled and shocked, yes, but not scared. Instead, relief filled me—relief that he wasn't dead and that I hadn't been dreaming about a dead man.

Hope seemed to be my second heaviest emotion. Hope that maybe my foolish fantasies hadn't been so foolish after all. Time would only tell about that, but as he followed me up the stairs, I found it difficult to look ahead rather than twisting my head the whole time to look at him.

He looked just as I knew he did—just as I'd painted him. Only it was an entirely different thing to see him in person. It was better. He, although I wouldn't have thought it possible, was even more handsome in person.

Orick stood a good six inches taller than I'd imagined, and his eyes were a deeper shade of blue. It looked like the ocean when you stare down at its depths from out in the middle of its deep waters—a shade of blue that can't be captured in any sort of crayon or stained glass window.

I realized as I walked ahead of him that I couldn't even recall the clothes he wore. Was he in jeans and a sweater? Shorts and a t-shirt? Naked? *No, definitely not naked*, I thought to myself. I had to swallow to keep from laughing under my breath. I would have noticed if he were naked. Whatever he wore, I'd not taken notice of it the entire time he stood in the doorway, but I could scarcely look back now. If I did, I knew I would only find some other excuse to touch him again. I'd done enough of that in the doorway and he probably already thought it was weird.

At least I now knew why I'd painted him, why I'd seen him in my dreams for so many months—something meant to warn me that I would play a part in helping this man reunite with those he'd lost. It was a daunting task and one that I didn't feel equipped to handle, for I knew the shock and adjustment for both Orick and everyone else that thought him dead would be huge. Thank God I had Anne and, as soon as he was free from his charade tonight, Aiden, to help me manage and decide what was best.

For now, the only realistic thing for me to do was to take him back to my bedroom and talk things over with him and Anne, see if he needed anything, and see if he had a preference as to how we handled all of this.

It didn't take long to get to my room but, remembering back on Anne's ghost comment right as we reached the door, I realized I better warn her before strutting inside with him. I turned to face him and made a point to look over his clothing as I did so. It wasn't what I expected.

"I'm sorry, I know this is a rude question but…have you been homeless for a while? I'm just asking due to your manner of dress."

He wore dark, fitted pants but they were worn and dirty, and his shoes looked like they belonged in a museum. His shirt fit him loosely and had multiple holes. Everything was soaked through from the rain. Now that I wasn't so distracted by his eyes or his height or the way my heart seemed to squeeze erratically every time I touched him, I could see every curve of his muscular chest through the thin fabric of his shirt. It was stupid pretty.

After goggling him, I looked up to await his answer. He seemed entirely confused by my question.

"I doona ken what ye mean by either yer question or yer statement of my clothes. I'm sorry if the condition of them offends ye."

Immediately, I felt like an ass and hurried to assure him that wasn't the case at all.

"Oh no, not at all. I'm sorry. I shouldn't have said anything. Would you mind waiting right out here a moment? I have a friend inside. I think it's best I warn her about you before I bring you inside."

"Does she know me?"

I smiled, disappointed that I couldn't tell him yes after seeing the hope in his eyes.

"No, but she knows of you. She's heard talk of you, at least. It will just take me a second."

I stepped inside quickly and shut the door quietly behind me. Anne jumped away from the window, her mouth full of pizza as she spoke.

"So....did you find him and give him a piece of your mind? I was trying to watch, but I couldn't see or hear anything."

"It wasn't Adwen."

"It wasn't?"

"No. Are you sober enough to not freak out when I tell you who is on the other side of that door?"

She swallowed and nodded as she crossed her arms and sat down on the edge of my bed.

"Yes, Gillian. I didn't have that much wine, and the pizza helped. Don't tell me it's the ghost."

There was humor in her voice but, when I didn't laugh or deny it, her tone changed considerably.

"Gillian?"

"No, it's not a ghost, but it is the man we thought was a ghost."

She stood and marched over to the door to open it. I stepped in her way.

"You've got to be gentle with him. This is all a lot for him, I think. He doesn't remember anything."

"No?" Her voice was disbelieving.

"Yes. He really doesn't, and I don't think he's been living under the best of circumstances. He's quite dirty. You'll see. Go ahead and open the door."

Anne didn't hesitate for a moment, and she reacted in a way much like I did—goggled at him a few long seconds before doing her best to recover before pulling him inside and shutting the door.

"Holy moly, you look just like your painting."

Orick's brows scrunched together as he looked down at Anne.

"My painting?"

I hurried to distract him. He would learn about the painting soon enough, but I didn't think it best to lead with it.

"It doesn't matter. Why don't you sit down? Want a piece of pizza?"

He sat as I instructed and looked at the cheesy pie as if I'd asked him to eat a live rat.

"What is pizza?"

The word sounded uncomfortable on his tongue.

"Oh boy, you don't remember much, do you? Eat it, you'll like it."

I could tell he was hungry for he dug in right away. Within seconds his face grew lax with delight.

"'Tis wonderful, truly. It puts my own cooking to shame. Marion's as well."

He mentioned Marion often and, whether it was out of gratitude or more, I couldn't tell but I knew that she meant a great deal to him. Although if he was truly unable to remember anything before her, she was probably the most important person in his life. I couldn't help but wonder why he left her. Knowing that we had more pressing things to discuss, I decided to file the question away to ask him at a later time.

"Orick, I don't want to overstep in any way, and I'm really not sure what is the best way to go about this, so I'll just tell you what I know and then you let me know if you have a feeling for how you'd like to proceed."

He nodded and kept his eyes locked right on me, ready to listen.

"Okay. I don't know you and neither does Anne, but I own this castle and…"

"I'm sorry." He interjected, and I fell silent. "Ye are laird of this castle? Marion spoke of the laird and said he was a man, no a lassie."

"What? No, I'm not laird. Lairds don't really exist in Scotland anymore. They haven't for a very long time."

I watched his reaction closely, trying my best to read him. Losing his memory was one thing, but the question made me worry for him even more. What if he'd lost touch with far more than that and with his memory his mind had gone as well?

He thought on my answer for a long moment then shifted in his seat as he seemed to accept my words.

"Marion may not know. She doesna live among people so I confess to no knowing myself. Carry on, lass."

"Okay, well I own this place, and a family is renting it from me for just a few nights. I believe that they know you, though I'd rather not go into why I think that right now, but I'm certain they do. They thought you were dead, and I know it will come as a shock to them to see you."

"Aye, I'm sure it will."

I glanced over at Anne who stood leaning against the door of my bedroom, her arms crossed, as she silently took in our exchange. I hoped she would voice the perfect solution but as I watched her, I knew that she considered herself an onlooker in the strange exchange, not an active participant. I was on my own.

"I don't think tonight would be the best time to spring it on them. Would it be okay with you if we wait until morning, give me a chance to talk to them and then bring you all together?"

Voices from downstairs suddenly seemed to approach my bedroom, and we could all tell that a commotion of sorts was taking place downstairs. Anne quickly stepped out into the hallway to check on things. A few seconds later, she re-entered with a very frustrated Aiden at her side.

He was visibly drained and so frustrated that he didn't even notice Orick sitting at the small table by the door.

"I am a fool to have signed up for that mess. I think they bought it, but I havena been in a room with that much palpable angry tension since our wedding, Anne. And then, it was only because you were angry at your sister for wearing white. That old man is a crazy, hateful bugger."

Aiden stood with his back toward Orick while he talked to Anne and didn't stop talking for some time.

"I canna imagine why Jane and Grace went to all this trouble for his benefit. Why, the way he talked to ye and Gillian…I wanted to punch him in the teeth. He's left, along with the old woman. They dinna like that Grace refused to send Cooper back with them for schooling in the States, and they left in a heated fury of curse words. Why the poor lad certainly learned a few words to toss around the school yard this night."

Anne, who clearly didn't know how to address everything Aiden said, just responded as if Orick and I weren't there.

"Oh, that's terrible. Everyone gone off to bed then?"

"On their way there. I know that ye meant to stay up with Gillian so the two of ye can pretend like yer fourteen again, but I need ye with me. The whole evening was too much for me to take."

I decided to interrupt before he made everyone uncomfortable with further bedroom talk.

"It's fine, Aiden. You can take her, but first, I think there's someone you should meet."

He spun quickly. His face gave way to his embarrassment for one quick second before he saw Orick. Then, his eyes turned to horror, and he backed into Anne and knocked her flat on the ground.

I rushed over to help her up as Aiden stuttered and sputtered his words.

"Wha…It…I…Gillian, I told ye to no go speaking about ghosts. Ye invited him in ye did."

Anne, once standing, laughed and rubbed her husband's back gently.

"He's not a ghost, you silly man. He's just not dead like everyone thought."

The fear in Aiden's face dissolved at once as he spoke to Orick.

"Oh. Well, good on ye then. I suppose ye are glad about that."

Then, with as much matter-of-fact attitude as I'd ever seen from him, Aiden turned to address me, an ornery twinkle in his eye.

"Gillian, I think I've dealt enough with this family tonight. This bloke here and whatever ye mean to do with him, is on ye. I'm going to take my wife to bed and intend to stay there until the whole lot of them have left."

I started to protest but he didn't give me much chance, swinging Anne over his shoulder as if she weighed nothing at all. I called after her for help but apparently, a night spent making love to her husband was more appealing to her than the complicated situation that sat in my bedroom. All she did was lift her head and wink at me as they walked out the door and closed it behind them.

Orick and I were now all alone.

Chapter 12

I allowed him to finish off the pizza. Despite the rumbling in my stomach, I imagined that he needed it far worse than I. He didn't say much as he ate and that suited me just fine for it allowed me a few moments to think on how the rest of the evening would progress.

I knew that I couldn't very well place him in a spare room with the way Cooper ran about and did as he pleased, and I couldn't stay somewhere else for the very same reason. So, with no other solution that I could see, it seemed we would have to share a room for the night.

He also needed to be cleaned. While a shower would be easy enough with a bathroom now connected to my room thanks to Aiden's modernized restorations, I didn't have any clean clothes to give him. At first I thought about running down to Aiden and Anne's room but then thought about the glint in Anne's eyes as they'd left and thought better of it.

After that, I would just put him to sleep and allow him a good night's rest before the overwhelming events that were bound to occur tomorrow.

"Might I ask yer name, lass? Ye were kind enough to give me my own. I'd like to know yers as well."

I couldn't believe I'd overlooked sharing that with him before.

"Of course you can ask it. It's Gillian. My name is Gillian."

He tested the name out by mouthing it before he said it.

"Gillian. 'Tis a bonny name. Might I ask ye a few others."

I smiled and nodded while I handed him a cloth napkin so he could wipe the remaining pizza crumbs and sauce from his fingers and mouth.

"Are ye married, Gillian?"

"No." I laughed and gestured around the room. "Do you think I'd have you sitting inside my bedroom if I was?"

He smiled sheepishly. I didn't miss how his cheeks reddened at the implication of my words. "Aye well, fair enough. Do ye know…do ye know if I am married?"

The thought, in all honesty, had never occurred to me. Not while I'd dreamt of him and certainly not once I'd seen him in the flesh. I hoped that he wasn't. But a man that looked as he did, with such a kind way about him…how could he not be married?

"I don't know. You'll find out tomorrow, I guess. Have you had enough to eat? If you're still hungry, I can slip downstairs to the kitchen and round something up for you."

I secretly hoped he would say yes just so I'd have an excuse to get myself something to eat as well. He quickly turned down my offer.

"Oh no, lass. I've already eaten more this night than I have in many days. I'm just so pleased to no eat fish that I doona think I could eat another bite. Thank ye for all that ye've given me though."

I tried to hide my disappointment as I talked over the growl of my stomach.

"It's no problem. Do you want to get cleaned up?" I saw the discomfort on his face and knew that I'd worried him again—that I'd made him think I was insulted by his manner of dress or offended by his cleanliness. I quickly made haste to clarify my question. "Not that you need it. A shower just feels very nice sometimes when you're tired. The new hot water heater works very well."

"Aye, I wouldna consider it kind of me to stay inside yer lovely home covered in dirt as I am, though I doona wish for ye to bring water up for me. If ye will show me where, I can do it myself."

"What? There's no bringing water anywhere. Come over here."

I waved him over and into the bathroom. Once he stood near me, I opened the shower door and turned on the water.

"See? The water just comes. Seeing it now, do you remember how to work it?"

I twisted to look at him, and I could see recognition flicker in his eyes as he grinned.

"Aye, it seems verra strange to me, but I believe I do know how. 'Tis almost as if I've stood under such a spray before."

I couldn't resist a small giggle and, turning off the water, I flicked the drips from my fingers at him playfully.

"Well, I should sure hope so."

"Marion dinna have one, though she dinna have much of anything. I bathed in the fishing hole among the rocks and the caves. I canna tell ye in a way ye might understand. It feels as if I have memories hidden from two separate worlds. One in which

Marion's cave seems a fine sort of home and the fire where we cooked our daily fish was more than suitable. In the other, a warm waterfall such as this seems the only reasonable way to rid yerself of dirt. Even the way ye have things lit is no strange to me. Does it make any sense to ye, what I mean?"

It didn't, not really, but I tried to take a guess at what he meant.

"Do you mean that while your memories of people and things that have happened is gone, you still understand the way things work? All of your skills, all of your common sense has remained?"

He nodded and shrugged, and I knew then that I'd missed the mark. Still, he remained polite and agreeable.

"In a way, though everything seems more at odds with each other in my mind. I only hope that when I see those who know me, the memories will come back to me. I doona believe they are gone for good for 'tis as if I can feel them lying in wait below the surface of my skin. If only I could scratch deep enough, they might rise to the top."

It made me ache for him, for the misery he must feel at being lost for so long. I could think of little worse than losing my memories, even the worst of them. For every single one was an integral part of who I was.

"I can't imagine what that must be like for you. I'm sorry for it. I'm sorry that this has happened to you."

"Ach, doona feel sorry for me. I doona feel sorry for myself. We each have our trials. This is mine."

"I suppose so. Now," I stepped out of the bathroom to give him some privacy. "I'll leave you alone to get cleaned up. I'm afraid I don't have anything for you to wear though. You'll have to…" In mid-sentence, I noticed my dark green robe hanging on one of the hooks in the bathroom and moved to lift it up and open to gauge its size.

It swallowed me whole and, as I looked it over, I imagined it would fit around him well enough, though it would need to be a good foot longer to be a decent length for him. Still, it would cover his most intimate bits. And if it didn't, I guessed I would just have to suffer the torture of catching a glimpse of his rear end.

"Why don't you put this on when you get out of the shower until the clothes you have on now are dry."

He looked at it suspiciously, but then stepped toward me causing his shoes to squeak from the way they were soaked through. Taking a glance down at his still-wet clothes, he relented and reached his hand out for it.

"Verra well. Thank ye."

The moment I shut the door to the bathroom, I heard the shower start to run and the soft sound of his clothes dropping to the floor.

"Did ye roll onto the floor, lass? Why else would ye no be in yer own bed?"

The sound of Orick's voice startled me, and I jumped up from my pallet on the floor so quick that my head spun as I stood. I only meant to prepare my mat for sleeping and instead fell asleep within a matter of moments.

"No, I didn't roll off the bed. I left it open for you."

He looked ridiculously adorable in my robe and nearly did give me a peek of his jewels when he puffed his chest out in reaction to my explanation for being on the floor.

"Do ye mean to tell me that ye intend for me to stay here with ye? In yer room? I couldna shame ye in such a way, lass. 'Twas fair different in the cave than here."

"Oh, come on now, Orick. I'm flattered that you're worried about my reputation, but don't be such a prude. You need a good night's rest. I insist that you take the bed. I've got plenty of blankets right here. It's pretty comfy actually. But you do have to stay here with me. We can't risk you staying in any other room. Not until they've seen you."

"No, lass. I willna have ye sleep on the floor."

He walked over to the bed and pulled at the top blanket, setting it down on the other side of the bed before he disappeared from view as he lay down on the floor.

I rolled over and looked at him from underneath the bed.

"What's the point in this? If you sleep on the floor, I sleep on the floor, too. I'm very stubborn. You do not want to try me on this."

He looked over at me, and one corner of his mouth pulled up in an appreciative smile.

"So what are ye saying? That if I want ye to sleep in the bed, I must sleep with ye?"

It did make me seem like a hussy, but I'd been raised to be a better hostess than that. I simply wouldn't stand for him to sleep on the floor just as he wouldn't allow me to either.

"No. I would prefer that you just get in the bed and let me lay here, but if you won't without me being in it, it's not going to hurt me any to share it with you."

"Are ye no worried that I'll take advantage of ye? That the temptation of ye lying next to me would be too much?"

I laughed and pushed myself up as I dragged the blankets from my pallet back onto the bed. I knew what my hair most likely looked like now that I'd fallen asleep on it, and I also knew the sounds I made in my sleep—neither were attractive. Even if I'd been with a man far less polite, I wouldn't have been too worried about me presenting myself as a temptation—not that I intended to place myself in such a situation with strange men ever again.

"I'm not worried. Should I be? You don't strike me as the type."

"No, lass. I swear that I willna touch ye."

Seeing that I meant every word, he slowly followed my lead, rolling the blanket he'd pulled from the bed into a long snake that he lay down its middle as a sort of separation between the two of us.

After I flipped off the lights, we both settled in the bed a comfortable distance from the other, and I started to drift just as quickly as before when Orick's voice spoke to me in the darkness.

"I'm frightened, lass."

We lay with our backs to one another but, recognizing that he needed someone to talk to, I twisted toward the center at the same time he did, placing our bodies much closer to one another. Seeing him that way, lying so close to me that I could feel the heat of his breath, reminded me so much of my dreams of him that I wanted to reach for him, to pull him close to me and press my lips against him. I almost did just that but saw sense when he opened his mouth to speak again.

"I believe that I'll remember with time, but that time may no be tomorrow. I doona wish to cause those who know me pain."

Instead, I rested my palm on the side of his cheek to comfort him.

"You needn't be worried about that. All of it will come as a shock to them so know that, but if they love you, they will give you the time you need."

He said nothing. All I could see were his blue eyes in the moonlight.

"You know…" I whispered the words to him as I scooted just slightly closer, the front of my body bumping the barrier he had created between us. "I know you may not remember this but sometimes to give someone courage you press your lips against another to pass on that strength to them. I have some to spare, if you'd like it."

He smiled in the darkness, and I didn't allow him the chance to answer before I leaned in and brushed my lips ever so softly against his own. I didn't linger long, but his hand rose to my cheek and cupped it as he guided me to his face for a second kiss. His touch was light and gentle, and it was over as quickly as it had begun.

With that, I rolled over and bid him goodnight.

He said nothing, but I could tell that he knew I lied.

Chapter 13

For the first time since moving into the castle, I didn't dream about Orick. I dreamt of my parents and how much I missed them. It was the kind of dream where the memories are so acute you can smell them, touch them, hear them, even see them in a way that makes your heart ache from the sudden longing you feel at missing them. When I woke, tears lingered in the corner of my eyes.

I twisted over my shoulder to make sure Orick still slept before slipping out of bed and into the bathroom where I could wash the tears and memories away with a hot shower. I didn't dream about them as often as I once did, but the significance wasn't lost on me.

They were like beacons, lighthouses, leading me either toward or away from something I couldn't yet see myself. Reminding me of their wisdom when I was in need of it, even long after they were gone. My dreams of them had always been that way.

What were they trying to tell me now, I wondered? Perhaps it was a simple sign of their approval of Tracy's decision to give me the castle. Whatever it was, I never knew how to feel about such dreams. In a way, I never wanted them to end but, once they did, I always wished they'd never happened. The feeling of being so unattainably close to them always just made me hurt and, more often than not, cry.

I allowed myself those tears while I showered but once I finished, I let them wash away with the suds that ran down the shower drain.

I readied myself in the bathroom, doing the job quickly and moving around as quietly as I could so as not to wake Orick. I managed to get the job done pretty efficiently, and I was basically finished when I heard the bed creak as if he'd stood. I opened the door to see him standing, and I had to call out to him to keep him from stretching upward in my little shortie robe while I looked on.

"Morning, let me just close the door before you do that. Otherwise, I'll get a nice wide shot of your rear end."

He stood with his back toward me but laughed at my words.

"'Tis more likely to embarrass ye than me, lass."

He turned and pointed to the bed. "'Twas the best night's sleep I can remember."

"Good." I stepped and moved to make the bed now that he was standing. "I think you needed it."

He immediately moved to help though I could tell it was a task he wasn't overly familiar with as he mimicked my moves exactly. Not that I put that off to his memory loss—he was, after all, a man.

"I believe I did. For the first time since my fall, I dinna dream of senseless colors and voices."

"That's good. What did you dream?"

I knew that for me, my dreams often pulled from my own memories of things I'd seen. I wondered what a man with so few memories would dream about.

He smiled and looked down at his feet rather shyly.

"I doona know if I should tell ye but 'twas of ye, and it dinna feel like a dream, lass. It felt like a memory. Are ye sure ye doona know me?"

"I'm sure. I would have told you if I knew you. But maybe that means you are starting to remember and your mind just replaced someone else's face with my own because you'd just seen me before you went to bed. I think that's good news."

"Hmm."

He made the noise as he stepped away from the bed and crossed his arms as he thought.

"Mayhap ye are right, but I could see ye with such detail, Gillian. I stood out in the rain, just outside yer bedchamber window next to a lass I couldna see. I watched ye as ye stood there, yer red hair covering half of yer face. I watched ye, but ye couldna see me. How desperately I wanted to know ye."

I swallowed and the room seemed to warm suddenly with his words.

I stuttered over a few unsure words and nearly collapsed with relief when the handle to my room rattled as if someone meant to enter. It kept me from trying to follow up his dream confessional with any sort of reply, which was good because my heart was pounding way too hard for me to do so successfully.

Anne I could deal with and speak to just fine. I assumed she meant to check in on us after abandoning me the night before.

"I'm coming."

I walked over and opened the door to see Cooper standing in the doorway. In panic, I closed the door in his face as I turned to Orick.

"Step back out of the way for a minute and let me deal with him. I can't let you meet him until I've talked to the adults."

"Who is it?"

He did as I asked, but his curiosity was evident.

"It doesn't matter. Just stay back."

I opened the door once again and looked down at the child's wounded expression.

"Good morning, Cooper."

"Morning. Why'd you close the door in my face?

"Uh…" I stood in the crack of the doorway making sure he couldn't see inside. "My room is just a mess. I didn't want you to see it."

"Oh, my room is always a mess so you shouldn't worry about that. I brought you some coffee."

He extended a big, steaming mug in my direction, and I took it gladly.

"Thank you. That's so nice of you. I'll enjoy every drop." I stepped back into the room and started to close the door, but he stuck his foot inside to stop me.

"Hey, wait a minute. Is it okay if I come in? I could really use somebody to talk to."

I immediately felt sorry for him. "Oh. Is your Aunt Jane up? I'm sure she'd love to talk to you. You two are pretty close, right?"

His shoulders dropped. I knew my dismissal hurt him, but I didn't see another choice.

"I can't talk to her—not about last night. It was so awful, Gillian. They were all screaming at each other, and it was all about me. I hated it."

"Gillian."

The second voice was Orick's, and I gasped at the urgency of it.

"Who was that?"

Cooper tried to step around my legs, but I held him back.

"Nobody. Hang on just a second."

I shut the door as much as I could and looked back over at Orick with wide, aggravated eyes, but the moment I saw him, my anger vanished. I knew before he spoke what he would say. I could see in his eyes that he'd changed.

"Gillian. What is the lad's name?"

"It's Cooper."

"Let me see him. His voice…I know it."

Chapter 14

How would it feel to remember? He thought it would be painful, like a flooding of his mind with so many feelings, images, and memories that it would be difficult to take or understand.

His expectations were so different than the way it happened.

Instead, when he stood beside the door and heard the young boy's voice, he simply knew how to talk to him, knew what would make the lad feel better. And then, when Gillian stepped away from the doorway and he saw the boy, it seemed as if he'd never forgotten.

He knew him, he loved him, and he remembered every game of hide-and-seek he'd ever played with the boy, every surprising thing that came out of the lad's mouth. In an instant, the man he'd been for many moons vanished, replaced by the man he truly was.

"Cooper."

The boy charged him, jumping toward Orick as he reached his arms down to lift the child. He smiled as Cooper's little arms squeezed tightly around his neck.

The child's faith astounded him. He didn't look at him with fear, doubt, or confusion—none of the emotions that he knew Jane would have when she saw him for the first time in so much time. No, Cooper simply saw him and believed that his eyes saw the truth, and it was enough for him to let joy overtake him. A joy so strong that Cooper's little body shook all over as he held him.

Tears filled Orick's eyes as he listened to Cooper sob into the collar of the robe he still wore, and he allowed the child the time they both needed as they treasured the first moments of their joyous reunion.

Eventually, the boy took a deep breath, holding in any other sniffles as he reared back in Orick's arms and placed his little hands on either side of Orick's face.

"We all thought you died. Oh, Orick, I'm so glad you didn't. I've missed you so much."

Cooper gasped at the end of his words and took to crying once more as Orick gathered him up and held him close.

"Ach, lad, I've missed ye as well. I'm sorry it took me so long to get back to ye. O'course it should be ye that would bring all the memories back for me. I've always thought ye possessed a wee bit of magic, what with yer wise soul and smart tongue. It seems I was right."

"What? What does that mean?"

"When I fell into the ocean…I dinna remember anything. No until this moment."

Cooper still held a firm grip on either side of his face.

"You didn't remember us? What have you been doing all this time?"

"I lived in a cave, I ate lots of wee fish, and I spoke to only one person—a kind but strange lass by the name of Marion. She saved my life."

Cooper finally released his face, moving his hands to rest on Orick's shoulders.

"Are you sure you remember everything now? What is my favorite color?"

Orick laughed and turned his head suspiciously at the child.

"I doona think ye've asked a fair question. Ye change yer mind all the time. One day 'tis blue, the next green, and still others ye enjoy red."

Cooper giggled and leaned in to give him a quick little hug.

"That's it! You do remember because I never know what to say to that question. Do you want to see Aunt Jane?"

He noticed right away that Cooper hadn't said Adwen's name, and he wondered if something had happened between them. He would find out soon enough.

"Aye, but first…"

He wasn't given the chance to finish as Cooper screamed at the top of his lungs.

"Aunt Jane…come in here right now! You're going to want to see this!"

"Ach, Cooper. I've already suffered a loss in memory, I doona wish to lose my hearing as well. Doona call for yer Aunt Jane yet. Best we approach them with the news slowly."

Gillian spoke to them from the doorway, and he allowed Cooper to twist in his arms so he could look back at her.

"I'll go and talk to them now. Why don't you two stay here?"

Once she was gone, Cooper wiggled from his arms and reached for his hand to pull him to the ground.

"Okay. Let's sit on the floor while she goes to get them. You know you look goofy, don't you? I'm pretty sure that's a girl's robe you've got on."

Orick laughed and slid down to the floor.

"'Tis. I dinna have any clothes when I came here. I dinna know I was going through the portal, for I dinna remember it. What are ye all doing here in this time, Cooper?"

"Morna sent Mom a letter when she heard that my grandparents were coming to Scotland. I guess they were pretty mad that it's been so long since they've seen me. So we had to come since they think Aunt Jane owns this castle and meet them here. It didn't go well."

"Aye, I heard that last night."

Cooper's voice sounded surprised.

"You've been here since last night?"

"Aye. What happened with yer grandparents?"

Cooper shrugged and looked down at the floor.

"They wanted me to go back with them to go to school in New York. They don't understand because they can't. And we can't tell them. They would never believe."

"I'm sorry, lad. 'Tis no always easy with families, though they all love ye."

"I know and it's okay. None of that can make me sad, not now that you're here."

Orick could hear the sounds of footsteps approaching, followed by Jane's raised and questioning voice. He stood to ready himself for Jane's entry. It didn't surprise him that Gillian's conversation with her hadn't lasted long. The moment

Jane heard such an outrageous claim, Orick knew she would need to see proof right away.

It grieved him to think on the day he almost died, how he fell helping Jane climb her way back to the top of the rocky hillside. He hoped she didn't carry guilt, didn't blame herself for all that had occurred. He certainly didn't.

"I don't know what you're playing at, nor am I sure how you even know about Orick. Haven't you ever lost anyone before? This is not a kind thing to tell someone. If Orick lived, we would have heard from him long before now. He wouldn't have stayed away."

Orick listened as Gillian's voice, much softer and less combative, trailed behind Jane's. He knew by the ceasing of their footsteps that they stood right outside the door.

"He couldn't remember anything. None of this is any of my business; I just thought it best to warn you before he walked into you in the hallway. See for yourself."

The door swung open. He watched Jane's reaction carefully, stepping toward her as she brought both hands to her cheeks in shock.

"How? Orick, how? You can't…you couldn't have…"

"I doona know how, lass, but I did. I canna tell ye how pleased I am to see ye."

Her face crumpled as she ran toward him.

Chapter 15

I slipped out quietly, thinking it impolite to intrude on such an intimate moment between two people as close as Orick and Jane. The moment I'd started in on what happened and that Orick was here, she stood and went in search of him, tearing into me every step of the way.

Not that I could blame her. It rattled her world in a way I couldn't even begin to understand. More than understand it, I couldn't feel it, couldn't empathize with it the way I knew I should have. It frightened me how easily I could close off emotions that other people felt so acutely.

Before I slipped out, as I stood there watching them with Orick's arms wrapped around Jane as she wept against his chest, I should have been moved to tears myself. Instead, I wanted to run.

It wasn't that I was completely void of human emotion. I worried about things; I enjoyed the company of others; I liked children and Christmas and sappy movies but, deep inside me, I'd grown cold. When it boiled down to seeing or feeling the most genuine forms of human emotion—fear, grief, intimacy, or love—I shut down.

In over a decade, the only person or thing that had really gotten inside me, that had wormed its way through the various walls I put up enough to really make me love them, was Toby, my loyal and loving dog. It was part of the reason dreams about my parents bothered me so much. They woke remnants of grief within me, and grief was an emotion I no longer allowed myself to feel.

Rather than think on them or talk about them, I expressed my feelings through a paintbrush and canvas. The images that I created there could never hurt me.

Even my recent dreams of Orick and the fanciful notion I allowed myself to think on—that he was my soul mate and we were destined to be together—I only did so when I knew it impossible that anything could come from it. Now that he was real and actually here, I couldn't allow myself to imagine such nonsense any longer.

The kiss had been an impulse and the very sort of thing I needed to do a better job of reining in.

I imagined Orick, Jane, and Cooper, along with the others when they made their way down to them, would need the day to talk things through and catch up on all that had happened. They could have all the time they needed. The castle was still theirs for another day. It meant I could get about my normal routine. After a quick game of fetch with Toby, I would retreat to the tower to paint.

"I think Anne drank more than she realized. She doesna feel so well this morning."

I continued to paint, waiting until Aiden stepped inside and in front of my vantage point to speak.

"Yes, well, she was downing it pretty fast. Have you been downstairs? Did you see that he's remembered?"

Aiden laughed and went to lean against one of the tall tower windows.

"I dinna know he'd forgotten, though Anne had no time to tell me anything after I got her inside our room."

I scrunched up my nose and made a noise of disgust.

"Keep it to yourself, will you? Do you want to start back on some work today? I'm sure you could work on our half if you wanted to."

"Aye, I already have, and I've called a handful of men to come in and help. I expect we've only six weeks left until we finish."

"That's great." I smiled but kept my eyes on my work.

"So...?"

Aiden never hovered. He was clearly very curious about something.

"So...what?" I clamped the paintbrush with my teeth as I reached to dab a smudge with the backside of my finger, making sure to not smear the rest of the paint.

"I came to check on ye. I'm sorry we left ye last night, but I couldna stand another moment of the mess. Are ye all right? It must have startled ye to see him after the dreams and the painting and thinking him dead."

His concern for me took me aback. I wasn't accustomed and never had been to someone worrying over me, but I knew that Aiden was just that way with everyone.

"I'm fine. It freaked me out way more when I thought he was dead, so now that I know he's not, I'm no longer worried that I'll wake up to see a ghost standing at the end of my bed."

"Aye, 'twould be a relief to me as well. What do ye think yer dreams were about then?"

I removed the paintbrush from my teeth and set it down. Clearly, the conversation wouldn't be over any time soon.

"Probably just something warning me that I would have to help him, I suppose."

"That is no what ye told me last we spoke of this."

I warmed all over with embarrassment.

"Oh, that. That was stupid. Please don't say anything to him about it. It was all very silly, really."

He nodded in agreement.

"Aye, 'twas, but that doesna mean that ye canna fancy the lad. If ye want my opinion, ye should do something about it. Ye spend too much time in this castle and are bound to spend much more now that the place is yers."

"I don't know the guy. He could be a total weirdo. He could be married or have children."

"He is no a weirdo. I can tell. And he doesna have children, and he is no married."

I didn't want to have this conversation with him so I picked up my brush once more and tried to look very busy as I spoke so that hopefully he would take the hint and leave. He didn't and eventually, I fell for his bait.

"Just how would you know that?"

"I just asked him. He doesna have himself a woman either. I can tell that he fancies ye. The whole time I spoke to him, he glanced about the room looking for ye."

I stood and moved to the doorway so that he would see I wanted him to leave. His suggestions were pointless. Orick would leave, and I would never see any of them again.

"Aiden, if he was glancing about the room, I doubt he was looking for me. He was probably looking for a way to escape you and your prying questions."

"Whatever ye say, Gillian, but if ye think I canna see the sort of person ye are, ye are wrong. I was much as ye are once. It took Anne to wake me up and make me see that it's important to let love in or if love is no possible for ye, at least allow yerself a fair deal of lovemaking. It's good for ye. When ye spend so much time pushing people and experiences away from ye, all ye end up with is yerself. With a mind like the one that ye and I have, that is no a verra pleasant place to be."

Chapter 16

"'Twas a day much like this one when we last walked across the castle grounds. Now that I have ye alone, allow me to ask ye a question, Jane. Did things end between ye and Adwen? Why is he no here with ye?"

He hoped Adwen wouldn't have done something so foolish as to let Jane go. The lass was Adwen's match in every way. If she answered *aye*, Orick would leave at once to track him down and beat some sense into the fool.

"Oh gosh, no." Jane linked arms with him as they walked. "We're married now."

"I am pleased to hear it, lass, though he doesna deserve ye. I am sorry that I wasna there to see it."

He took his free hand and gave Jane's a gentle squeeze as she sniffled. She'd cried on and off since seeing him.

"Don't be sorry. There's nothing for you to be sorry for. I'm the one that's sorry. I'm the one at fault for everything that happened. Every single day since you fell on those rocks, I've had to work to forgive myself for that. "

She broke down as Orick moved them to the steps in front of the castle. He pulled her toward them, wrapping his arms around her as she wept.

"I dinna die, Jane."

"But we thought you did, and we all grieved for you right up until this morning. Adwen still grieves for you every single day. Losing you was like losing a piece of his very soul. None of that would have happened if I hadn't been so stupid as to climb down those rocks."

"Jane, doona say another word about it. I dinna have to climb after ye. I wanted to. 'Tis the fault of no one. I willna listen to ye blame yerself for it again. I doona blame ye and neither does Adwen, I know it. So release the burden for yer own sake. Now, where is Adwen? I know him better than he does himself, and I know how much we mean to one another. I know he dinna take it well. He wasna easy for ye afterwards, was he?"

"No." Jane pulled away but held on to his hands as she spoke. "He wasn't, but I didn't expect him to be. He was here. He left yesterday not long before you arrived, I guess. You two probably came very close to crossing paths. He's gone to look for Lennox and Griffith. They seem to have gone off the radar on one of their trips."

Concern shot through him at such news. The MacChristys were seasoned on the road. If they didn't show up where expected, something unexpected delayed them.

"Ach, I should leave after them. I'll go at once."

He started to stand, but Jane stopped him by tugging on his arm.

"No, Orick. That's not a good idea. They all think you are dead. You can't just go riding up after them and scare them all to death. Besides, we've instructions to meet Adwen back at our home in McMillan territory. It's where we've settled so that I could stay close to Cooper. We still travel a lot but when we aren't, that's where we call home. Callum took over as laird of Cagair Castle shortly after your fall."

"Ye doona sound worried for them, Jane. It worries me greatly."

"It's not that. Of course I'm worried, but Adwen truly didn't seem concerned. I think he had an idea of where he would find them. Even if you left now, by the time you made it to them, it's likely they would be on their way back."

He knew she was right, but he didn't like the thought of staying here and doing nothing while Adwen and Callum worried over their father and brother.

Jane stood and motioned for him to follow her.

"We'll go back through tomorrow. Once we do, if you really still want to go after them, I'll accompany you. That is, of course, unless you want to see if Gillian wants to come along too."

Gillian—he knew now why she'd seemed familiar to him. She'd bewitched him long before when he'd seen her up in her window, just as he had in his dream the night before.

"O'course I canna ask her to come. I doona know the lass. 'Twould require that I tell her of the portal and when I truly come from."

"So?" Jane shrugged her shoulders. He wished he could always be as carefree as she. "She owns the place. It's probably best that she know about it, so no one staying with her ever wanders down there and disappears forever. Orick, do you not remember who she is? She's your lady, the one you pointed to that night in the window. I think you fell in love with her right then. I've never seen you react to anyone that way."

He remembered it all as if it were yesterday.

"How can I love someone that I doona know?"

"I knew very little about Adwen when I fell in love with him. I still don't know everything about him. I'm not sure that I ever will. But you sure won't know anything about her unless you spend some more time with her. Taking her back with us will certainly give you that."

He laughed and hoped that he would never again have to spend a day without seeing Jane. She always lifted his spirits.

"Aye, 'twould but might require kidnapping the lass. Surely ye doona wish for me to do that."

"Kidnapping her? Why would you do that? Just talk to her. Tell her. My guess is she will be curious enough to go even if she thinks you're crazy until she gets back there. Besides, I'm sure she likes you. Any woman with a pair of eyes and a normal sex drive would. Do you have any reason to think that she doesn't like you?"

Orick shook his head. The things that came out of Jane's mouth always leaned towards the inappropriate, and he loved her for it.

"No, I ken she likes me just fine. She kissed me."

"Kissed you? Already? Geez, that woman moves just about as fast as I did. I kissed you the first night I met you, too."

"I remember. It nearly brought me to my knees and Adwen as well. I doona think she meant anything by it."

Jane picked up her pace as she effectively led him back to the castle's back door.

"It doesn't always have to mean anything. That's a great start. Now go and talk to her. Then, come morning, when she thinks you're totally crazy for thinking you are from the past, we will take her back with us and scare the crap right out of her when she sees you were telling the truth."

Chapter 17

"Ye have a gift for that, lass. I told Aiden I would come and get ye. He's cooked the evening meal for everyone, though we asked him to no do so."

I could lose myself in painting. I would think only half an hour had passed, and I would look down at my watch to find that it had been three. When I heard Orick's voice calling me to dinner, I could scarcely believe it—surely I'd only ushered Aiden out of the tower moments ago.

"It can't be time for dinner already."

When I turned to face him, his brows were pulled together in confusion as he pointed out the windows to the darkened sky. He looked better out of my robe and the rags he'd arrived in, and he filled out what I could only assume were Eoghanan's clothes quite well.

"Aye, 'tis. Did ye no notice the sun set?

"No. I didn't. Time often gets away from me when I'm up here. I get pulled in to whatever I'm painting."

"Might I see yer other paintings? There is one in particular that wee Cooper told me of that has made me verra curious."

I didn't see any point in denying or keeping it from him.

"The painting of you, you mean? Sure. Here it is."

I walked over to the wall and flipped it outward so he could see it. He looked it over with great interest, saying nothing while he stared at it. Eventually, I couldn't take the suspense.

"What are you thinking?"

He turned his eyes toward me, and my face blushed immediately—it was the thing I disliked most about my fair skin. Everyone could always tell when I was embarrassed or nervous.

"'Tis an impressive likeness. How could ye have painted me when we only just met?"

I shrugged, knowing that no explanation would sound sane.

"I think something was warning me that you would show up at the castle. I've been dreaming about you."

"No, lass. 'Tis no the reason ye dreamed of me."

He stepped nearer to me, and I bumped into the windowsill as I stepped back instinctively.

"You don't think so? What was it then? Like you said, I didn't know you until yesterday."

He mirrored my position, leaning into the stone wall next to me with his shoulder so that we faced one another. He stayed a good distance from me as he spoke, helping to ease my nerves a little.

I knew there was no real reason to be nervous around him. Anyone could see the sort of man he was just by looking into his eyes. There was a kindness in them that gleamed with every expression and gentle authority in every step he took that made him trustworthy.

Still, my actions of the night before left me embarrassed. I didn't kiss men I didn't know. I didn't act so impulsively without thinking about the consequences of my actions. I didn't tend to do things without a point and, kissing Orick, what with him leaving and with my being so emotionally unavailable, was pointless.

"Ye could feel my wanting of ye. 'Tis why ye dreamed of me."

I swallowed hard as I replayed what he'd just said in my mind. He didn't seem the sort of man to be so forward, and I couldn't even begin to guess what he meant.

"What?"

"Do ye believe in magic, lass?"

My answer came out before I could soften the bluntness of my answer.

"No. Definitely not."

He surprised me by laughing as he pointed to the painting as if to support his case.

"How can ye no believe in magic when ye have proof of it right here?"

I stepped away from the wall and walked to the front of the painting.

"That is not proof of anything. Maybe proof that I'm slightly psychic or something, but I've always felt I was a little bit of that. I can sometimes feel things before they happen, but I don't ever have enough sense of them to really understand what they mean."

Orick's face took on a glazed look.

"I dinna ken what ye meant by a word of that. In truth, it doesna matter whether ye believe in it or no, for I know well enough that it exists."

"Okay, well that's fine. You're certainly entitled to your own opinions." I smiled and looked down at my feet while I searched for a way to change the conversation. "Now that you've remembered, congratulations on that by the way, can I ask what part of Scotland you're from? You speak quite differently from Aiden, what with all the *'tis-es* and the *kens*. You speak like Eoghanan and Adwen. Where do you all come from?"

He smiled, and I couldn't help but do the same as the corner of his mouth turned up. It was endearing and infectious.

"'Tis no a matter of where we are from, but when."

"Okay…clearly you are going to make me ask. What exactly does that mean?"

He surprised me by reaching for my hand. I allowed him to take it as I followed his lead down the stairs. He didn't answer me until we were near the bottom.

"Ye say that ye doona believe in magic. If I asked ye to allow me to prove it to ye, would ye allow me to do so? 'Twould require ye to accompany me on a journey."

I trusted him, but I also realized that such a trust was rather foolish. I didn't know him—he'd done nothing to earn my trust. And despite what I felt in my gut about him, scenes from criminal case television shows flashed in my mind at his question.

"A journey? Would this journey end with me shoved into the trunk of a car with duct tape across my mouth?"

Orick looked horrified and completely confused.

"Again, I doona ken, but I believe I can say no. Jane, Grace, Eoghanan, and all their children will accompany us. Allow me to show ye."

Curiosity got the better of me, and I knew I couldn't say no. Not only that, being around him seemed to make me impulsive.

Whether it was pointless or not, I wanted to spend more time with him.

"Fine. Show me."

"We will all leave come morning. Tonight, we shall all tell ye everything over the evening meal."

Chapter 18

Aiden and Anne looked entirely too calm. How were they not as shaken by everything as I was? It didn't make any sense to me at all.

"I'm going to repeat myself once again because obviously you guys weren't paying attention at dinner. They are convinced they live in the seventeenth century—every single one of them. How is that not certifiably crazy? I'm really half tempted to call someone, for Cooper's sake if nothing else."

Anne laughed and dismissed my concern with absolute certainty.

"Don't be ridiculous, Gillian. Cooper is the most levelheaded and well cared for child I've ever seen. If anybody needs to be called on, it's you. Just take a breath and think about everything that they said."

What was there to think about? The very idea that I was the one out of line or acting crazy baffled me completely.

"Aiden, back me up here. It's crazy, right?"

"No, I doona think so. Why doona ye go with them and see for yerself?"

I collapsed in frustration onto one of the couches in the sitting room.

"Are you telling me that you believe them?"

Anne came over and gave me a shove so that I would scoot over as she sat down beside me and looked up at Aiden.

"Should I tell her or should you? Which one of us is more likely to get through?"

Aiden smirked and pointed at Anne.

"I vote for ye. Yer American. Ye can relate to her close-mindedness and lack of belief in anything out of the ordinary."

Anne glared at him then turned to face me.

"Okay, Gillian, I'm going to tell you a story. I know you won't believe most of it, but at least listen. After I've finished, you can leave with Orick and the rest of them and see for yourself that I'm telling the truth. My hope is that with this story, you'll be able to understand why we believed them so easily."

I ground my teeth, crossed my arms, and settled in to listen to her fairy tale.

"Fine."

"I'm not sure how you thought Aiden got this job. I'm sure Tracy made it sound like she did it out of the goodness of her heart. I can assure you, that's not what happened."

I never believed Tracy did anything out of the goodness of her heart. Everything that Tracy did—good, bad, or indifferent—was in her best interest.

"No, I just assumed she hired him because she knew him from college and he does good work."

Anne winked at Aiden and smiled with pride.

"Both of those things are true but no, that's not why she hired him. Or at least, maybe that is why she hired him, but it's not as if she called him to inquire about the job. We had to come to her, and we wouldn't have even known about the possibility without the help of a little magic."

I kept my mouth shut, as promised, while I waited for her to continue.

"Two weeks before Tracy hired Aiden for this job, he was about to send all of his team members to look for work elsewhere. We were about to sell our house and were talking about moving to the States and living with my family for awhile to get back on our feet."

I would never have suspected that they were struggling in such a way. I reached out to squeeze Anne's hand.

"What happened?"

"You see how remote everything is here. It was hard to find work, and slowly our savings ran out. Anyway, right when we were ready to make the call, our phone rings and it's some old woman out in the middle of nowhere—a few hours outside of Edinburgh—who wants to have some work done in her kitchen. Aiden drives out there to meet her, some lady named Morna, and she's decided she doesn't need any work done after all."

Anne paused and looked at Aiden knowingly.

"I'm sure he was ready to throttle the lady, what with the hope it had given us and the hours he had to drive when we hardly had the gas money. Anyway, right as he's starting to leave, she tells him she's caught wind of a job that would be much bigger for him and proceeded to tell us about someone buying Cagair Castle and putting up the money to restore the place. He could hardly believe it when she said Tracy's name. He called her right away and, by that night, he had the job, a job that was guaranteed for at least eight months and where he would make enough money to pay himself and his workers enough to last them well over a year."

Job tip aside, the situation would have frustrated me if I was in his shoes. Why would the old lady have him drive all the way out there just to change her mind?

"Why didn't she call and tell Aiden she didn't want work done and give him the tip on Cagair Castle anyway?"

Anne nodded and smiled as if I were finally catching on.

"That's exactly what I said. It didn't make sense. Regardless, I thought we owed her a thank you for the tip. It was one of those days where I was feeling rather cooped up anyway, and Aiden was already hard at work making plans for Cagair, so I decided to drive out to Morna's house myself and thank her in person. Aiden gave me very specific directions. When I got there, the house was completely gone, as if it never existed at all."

I couldn't stay quiet at that.

"Oh, come on now. You must have just gotten lost."

"No. I wasn't lost. I made sure of it. Then I made the long drive into Edinburgh and started asking around about her. My one-day trip out of the house ended up taking me three. I became sort of obsessed with finding her. Most people I asked had no idea what house I was talking about and had never heard of a woman named Morna who lived near Conall Castle. Then I finally found an old man who looked nearly as old as this castle is who said he'd heard stories about the disappearing house on the way to Conall Castle. Most people who have heard the story believe it's bad luck to see the house, for those that have usually disappear shortly after. For us though, it certainly hasn't been bad luck at all."

It was a rather remarkable story, but I didn't see how it was supposed to convince me that Orick and the rest of them weren't stark-raving mad.

"Is that all? It's a crazy story, Anne, I'll give you that. It's more than a little creepy, but I don't know—" She interrupted me mid-sentence.

"Don't you remember the name of the woman Jane said sent her and her sister back? The woman who dropped off their luggage and seems to play a large part in their journeys back and forth? Her name was Morna."

Now that Anne said it, I did remember Jane going on about the supposed witch named Morna, but at the time my brain had already overloaded and I'd not taken in much of what she said.

"So you think this witch that got Aiden the job is also somehow connected to our guests?"

Anne threw up her hands as if it were obvious.

"That's exactly what I think. Rumors of disappearances have happened at Conall Castle, at McMillan Castle, and here at Cagair as well. You remember how convinced Aiden was that he saw them crawling out of the cellar? Maybe it wasn't the drugs. Maybe he really did see that and that's where they travel back and forth. Maybe it's a thing with Scottish castles, and our guests are some of the very people that went missing. Maybe they went through and liked it. Let's be honest, we've seen their husbands so we know that's a definite possibility. They fell through somehow, fell in love, and decided to stay there and make lives for themselves. Maybe you're supposed to be the next missing person."

"The next missing person? That sounds terrible."

Anne stood and reached down to offer me a hand so she could pull me up right along with her.

"I think it sounds romantic. And you're going. There's no harm in seeing. My money is on them. They're telling you the truth, Gillian, and you're about to be in for one hell of an adventure, I expect."

Of course I would go. Even if they were crazy, hearing them talk about it over dinner had never really made me not want to go. All it did was make me think that I would need to have some sort of escape plan before I left with them just in case they turned out to be half as crazy as they all sounded.

"We will see, I guess. Are you and Aiden going to come?"

Now that we were both standing, Anne moved to Aiden's side, smiling as he placed his arm around her in a statement of joint agreement.

"Oh gracious, no. Of course we aren't going. Are you crazy? I am way too attached to sweat pants, movie night, and wine, but you go and have a great time. We will definitely come and see you all off though."

It seemed everything was decided, and I would have to get on board despite any monumental doubts I now had about the sanity of everyone inside Cagair Castle. We weren't leaving until morning. I assumed the only thing I could do before then was to get Toby and me all packed for what was sure to be one of the shortest and most ridiculous, imaginary trips ever.

One question hung in my mind as I carried Toby back up to my room—what did one pack for a trip to the seventeenth century?

Chapter 19

"Knock. Knock. Sorry to disturb you. Nobody has seen you in awhile, so I just thought I would drop in and check on you and bring you something that you can put on in the morning."

Jane stood in the doorway with Cooper as she looked at my suitcases and the various items surrounding them spread out all over my bed. A simple gray gown lay draped over her arm. Admittedly, it did look extremely out of place in this time, but as far as I was concerned, that didn't mean that it had come from another.

"Packing a few things, I can see. Do you mind if I help you with that?"

I could see that she intended to help regardless of what I said, so I smiled and nodded as they both walked all the way inside. Cooper didn't hesitate a moment as he crawled on top of the bed, right up in the middle of everything, and gathered a squirmy Toby into his arms. The pup took to wagging his tail and licking Cooper's face right away.

"He likes you."

Cooper smiled and nudged his own nose with Toby's.

"Good, 'cause I sure do like him."

Jane reached for one of my empty suitcases and went to close it, hesitantly pulling it off the bed as I watched her suspiciously.

"I don't mean to disappoint you, but you can't bring these suitcases with you. It wouldn't do for someone to see you rolling around something like this. I have a different sort of bag you can put a few things in, more of a pack sack of sorts."

I tried not to frown as I watched her roll my suitcase to the other side of the room.

"A pack sack?"

"Yes, a small cloth thing. You'll see. And good on you for thinking of laying out everything you'll miss, but you can't bring most of this stuff with you."

"Like what?" I sat down next to Cooper on the end of the bed and waited for Jane to take control.

"Well, toilet paper for starters. I know it would be great to have, but there's not really anywhere to put the stuff when you're done with it. It would just get really gross. You won't need shampoo either, but you won't really miss that. I'll admit, any time I come back here I always relish a good scrubbing with the stuff, but just wait until you get to use the oil mixtures that some of the ladies in McMillan village make. It's lovely, and your hair will shine and become so soft that you won't miss the suds as much as you would think. Is it all right if I gather up the things you definitely will want?"

I shrugged, knowing full well that she would do as she wished. Cooper obviously could tell the same thing, for he squirmed his way off the bed and turned to pet Toby as he spoke.

"This looks like it could take awhile. I think I'll go play downstairs. Would it be okay if I brought Toby with me? I promise I'll take good care of him. We will stay inside."

Toby jumped off the bed as if he understood every word and took off out the bedroom door ahead of him.

"I know you will. Absolutely. He will love that."

Once Cooper was gone, Jane waved for me to stand and watch over her shoulder.

"Grab all the toothbrushes and tubes of toothpaste you have. All of the modern girls I know back there, myself included, haven't been willing to give that up. We've even got our husbands using them, though we have to do that in private. Also, pick out one of your most comfortable lounging outfits. I keep a pair of modern clothes locked away in a sacred place and, if I ever find myself all alone, I am out of my dress and into my stretch pants in record-setting time. You'll want to do the same. Lastly, gather up a bunch of your modern undergarments. The guys love them and, since no one really sees them, I don't think there's any harm in feeling more like yourself. And trust me, having those on underneath the clothing we usually have to wear helps a lot."

It pleased me to hear her say that I could bring some of the things I'd already gathered. When she first started in, I assumed she was about to shelf everything. Still, she made it sound as if I would be gone a very long time.

"Just how long do you think I will be gone? You make it sound like it will be forever."

Jane smiled, leaned over and pushed all of my stuff to half of the bed, and sat down as she patted the bed for me to join her.

"Gillian, I'm sure you will come back occasionally just as we do, but I honestly expect that once you go through, you will never live on this side of time ever again."

I gulped down the anxious knot that rose in my throat at her words.

"Just why would you think that?"

"You're going to fight this, I can tell. Let me tell you now, as a former champ at battling this thing, there's no point."

Spending time with these people made me feel as if I came from another planet. They always spoke of things as if I should understand them, as if I should pick up on what they meant. I never did.

"What thing?"

"The love thing. That's what all of this is about—the time travel stuff. That's the point of all of it. It's why Morna still continues to live way, way past her expiration date. It's why each and every woman that has gone through has done so, and it's why you dreamt of Orick long before he showed up here."

"Whoa now." I jumped off of the bed like she'd poked me with a hot iron. "I'm just going on this trip out of pure curiosity. Nothing more. I feel like maybe you've gotten the wrong impression about Orick and me somewhere. I don't know him. I just helped him the night he arrived because he needed it."

Something flashed in Jane's eyes, and I knew even before she spoke that I upset her.

"No, don't do that. I didn't get the wrong impression about anything. You kissed him, didn't you? And you do like him, yes?"

"I…" I hadn't been so embarrassed or flustered since elementary school. I normally wasn't the sort of person to be so easily intimidated. I could hold my own in a heated debate, but emotions were like my kryptonite. To hear someone else talking about how I felt for someone else—it made me immensely uncomfortable. Still, she'd called my bluff and would know if I lied. "Yes, I did kiss him and I do like what I know about him, but I regret the kiss. I shouldn't have done that. I feel rather guilty about it."

"Guilt is a useless emotion. Trust me, I've had to learn that one for myself, and it wasn't easy. Don't waste your time on it. If you wanted to kiss him, then you were right to do so. Just don't play games with him. Not Orick. He deserves that less than any man I know."

"I'm not playing games with him. I'm just not very good at feeling-related things. Something's broken inside of me when it comes to connecting with others in terms of a relationship."

Jane surprised me by snorting as she gathered the small pile of things for me to take and stood with it as she walked to the door.

"I see. You're one of those, huh? That's good. Orick likes emotionally-stunted people. Otherwise, there's no way he could have remained my husband's friend for so long before he found me."

She laughed at herself, and I knew she teased.

"I'll put this stuff in a bag for you and bring it up. Best you get a good night's sleep. Cooper has already begged Orick to stay with him tonight, so we will see you in the morning. I'll bring Toby back to you when I bring your bag in a few minutes."

The next morning, I stood at the top of the hidden stairwell shocked for what I suspected would only be the first of many times that day. The cellar did exist and, despite all of my searching, I'd just simply been unable to find it. In my own defense, it was hidden incredibly well and, without someone as strong as Orick or Eoghanan to pull the stone door from its resting place, I doubted I would have been able to open it even if I had been able to find it.

"Are ye sure ye want to bring the wee dog along, lass?"

Toby wiggled in my arms, desperate to get free so he could run down the steps ahead of everyone. I tightened my grip at Orick's question.

"Absolutely. That's not up for discussion at all."

"Y-e-s."

Cooper dragged the word out, over-emphasizing the one syllable as he raised his fist toward the sky and then pulled it down in front of him triumphantly.

"I'm so glad he's going. I was going to be so sad to say goodbye to the little fellow."

Orick grinned and reached a shockingly large hand down to scratch Toby's head. How had I not noticed how gigantic his hands were before now?

"Aye, fine. I dinna expect for ye to say anything different. I enjoy the creature's company myself. 'Twill make it difficult though when we head for McMillan Castle, though I suppose the pup will do well enough. I only hope the horses take to him."

If the horses didn't take to him, I'd walk.

With that settled, Jane, who stood farthest down into the stairwell, turned to address everyone.

"Okay then, time to go I think. Grace and Eoghanan will go ahead with all the children first. Then the three of us will go along."

I pressed myself against the side of the stairwell, intent to watch every step Grace and her family took downwards. If they intended to play any sort of trick on me, I wanted to see it.

They didn't slow down as they reached the bottom, instead walking straight through the wall of stones at its base. One second they were there—the next they were not. My feet stepped backwards on instinct as everything in me wanted to run. Orick's hand touched my lower back, keeping me in place.

"Doona be frightened, lass. 'Tis no painful."

"Holy crap, Gillian." Anne spoke up from the top of the stairway. "They were telling the truth. I mean, I know what I told you, but I had my doubts of course."

If I was going to go through, I couldn't allow myself to think about it a moment longer. I turned toward Anne and Aiden as I took off down the steps, my small bag hanging on one arm and Toby held safely in the other.

"Okay, I'll see you guys in two weeks tops. Wish me luck."

I didn't wait for their goodbye as I closed my eyes and pushed through the remarkably un-solid wall.

Chapter 20

Orick didn't lie about the pain factor of the travel through. It shocked me at how little I felt. So much so that at first I didn't believe we'd gone anywhere at all. When we came out of the stairwell, Aiden and Anne were gone. Whether they intentionally left to give me a moment to acclimate myself or if they were just really ready to attend to their normal lives, I didn't know, but everyone save Orick scattered remarkably fast, leaving the two of us alone on the grass outside Cagair Castle. Even Toby leapt from my arms and took off after Cooper.

"So, I don't want to be a negative nay-sayer, but everything looks very much the same."

"No, lass." He neared me and placed his hand on my shoulder, pointing with his other as he directed me to look toward the road. "Do ye see that the road has gone? 'Tis no more than a worn path in the grass now, free of the rocks that were there before."

Remarkably, it was true. As I started to really look, I noticed there were in fact a great many differences. The stones of the castle looked visibly less worn, the stables off to the side still intact. In my own time, Aiden had yet to start work on them.

"Can I wander inside?"

"Aye, o'course. Look wherever ye wish. I'll follow yer lead."

If the stables and the lack of a real driveway weren't enough, stepping inside the doorway of the castle cured me of any remaining doubt. As unlikely and impossible as it seemed, I was most definitely not in the twenty-first century.

The first giveaway inside was the lighting. No modern lights were hung, no electrical outlets placed discreetly in the walls. Instead, candles and windows provided the only sources of light. It took me a long while, even in the middle of the day, for my eyes to adjust to the drastic change in lighting.

I made my way from room to room slowly, marveling at how remarkably similar but different things looked. It said a lot for the work Aiden had done, for the restorations were impressively accurate, only updated with the modern conveniences that were so obviously lacking in it here.

I saved my own room, or at the least the room that was mine some several hundred years in the future, for last. When I stepped inside, regardless of the time period, it still felt like mine.

"If ye'd like, I can take ye to the village. 'Twould have a fair number of things that ye would see there that might help convince ye of the truth."

My mind objected even before he finished talking. I couldn't handle any more shocking or strange sights for one day. I didn't need to see anything else to believe anyway. Not now that I'd seen the inside of the castle.

"No, thank you. This is enough. I believe you. I don't understand any of it, but I absolutely believe you. Orick," I waited for him to step closer, "tell me why you wanted me to come here. Surely it wasn't just so I would believe in magic."

He smiled and shook his head.

"No, Gillian. In truth, I doona really care what ye believe. I wish to spend more time with ye. 'Tis the truth of why I asked ye to come. I already care for ye more than I have right to."

He hesitated and in two long strides, before I could move, he reached me, gathering up both of my hands into his own. I wanted to lean into him at the gentle grip of his hands. They were rough and calloused but protective and kind. They were the hands of a man, a real honest-to-goodness man, that I had absolutely no business enticing into my crazy world.

"I am no a shy man, but I am also a man who lacks the familiarity of admitting my own desires, so forgive me if I'm too free with my declarations. I desire to learn everything about ye, Gillian, to understand the way ye think and what directs ye through life. I desire for ye to give me the chance to share the same parts of myself with ye. I only ask that ye give me time. If ye do, I know ye will love me in the end."

"Clearly, you're not lacking in self confidence either." I smiled and let loose a giggle so he would know I meant to tease him. I pulled one hand from his grip and rested it gently on his chest. "Orick, I wish I was the sort of woman who would be enough for you, but I know myself well, and I'm not. I could let you get to know me and you might just be the sort of person who would adore all of my strange habits and quirks, but when it came right down to it, I would never be able to love you back, not in the way you need. I don't feel things the way other people do."

Orick moved and held my hand against his chest with one hand while he brought his other to the side of my face and trailed my cheek lightly with his thumb.

"Ye may believe that of yerself but I doona. A lass who cares for any creature the way ye do for wee Toby is more than capable of loving in a way that would bring any man to his knees. I ken those who fear love well enough and doona doubt that I have more reason than most to fear it myself. I choose no to be frightened of the pain that might come from it."

He leaned in and pressed his lips gently against my forehead before crouching lower to whisper into my ear. My lips started to tremble as his breath shot down my neck.

"I wish to kiss ye. 'Tis time for ye to make yer own choice, Gillian. If ye push me away, I'll no try it again, and ye are free to return home. If ye allow it, I intend to destroy that fear of yers, to light it afire so it's no more than a distant memory and all ye have left is the dream and desire of love."

I could scarcely breathe, let alone make any move to stop him as he kissed me.

I know he meant it as a metaphor, but the heat of his kiss seemed to alight my whole body. I couldn't help but wonder if his touch would spark the flame meant to blaze away the fortress of fear around my heart.

I quit fighting as he moved his lips against me, leaning into him as he gathered me up in his arms.

Orick couldn't reach the stables fast enough after pulling away from his kiss with Gillian. It pained him to do so, but his need for her was too great for him to resist if he stayed in the room with her another moment. His breathing came rapidly, and he could think of nothing other than the way she felt pressed up against him. In truth, it had been no more than a kiss, but his body reacted in ways he'd forgotten it could.

Years spent at the side of the MacChristys, always balancing the line between friend and worker, had left him little time to explore the pleasures the rest of them feasted on gratuitously. To feel his heart pound in such a way that he could hear it beat in his ears was new to him. In that moment, his desire drove him rather than his heart or mind. He didn't wish to have Gillian that way, not until he had her whole heart.

"Did you just go for a run or something or are you having a heart attack? 'Cause you're sure breathing hard."

Orick sucked in one last deep breath as he regained composure and turned just outside the stables to find Cooper watching him curiously.

"Aye."

Cooper's brow pulled up in concern.

"Aye to what? Having a heart attack?"

"No, Cooper. I am no having a heart attack. Aye, I am breathing hard."

The child shrugged his shoulders in dismissal. "As long as you're not having a heart attack, I'm not worried. I came to tell you that my Mom and E-o went ahead and left with the babies since they would have to stop more than the rest of us."

"Aye, I imagined they would. And ye convinced Grace to let ye stay then?"

He smiled triumphantly. "Yeah, I told her that Gillian would probably need help with Toby."

"I'm sure she will be pleased ye are here to help her."

Cooper nodded, and Orick could tell from the look in his eye that he was up to something.

"Yeah, especially since Aunt Jane left with them."

"No, she dinna?" Orick knew the words Cooper would say before he said them. He knew exactly why Jane had decided to leave.

"She did. But she did it after Mom and E-o left so she could catch up with them after they were already too far gone to make her turn back here. That means it's just me, you, Gillian, and Toby. It's going to be so much fun. Why don't you go and tell her right now?"

Orick watched as Cooper skipped away. Fun it might be, but the journey would also be long. With the child, Gillian, and the dog, he expected the three-day journey to last them a fortnight.

Chapter 21

"Let's play a game, okay?"

Cooper's enthusiasm, even on our second day on the road, never seemed to dwindle. He jabbered and chatted and rode happily along come rain, shine, or the stalest of bread. The little fellow was a sight to behold. He sat astride his little horse confidently directing the creature with great skill. He wanted Toby to ride with him and, seeing as my horseback riding experience was minimal at best, I agreed right away. We easily fashioned him a sort of sling with which he could carry Toby close to his chest. The three of them made a remarkably adorable sight. I so hated that I didn't have my camera to take a picture of them.

Cooper's zest for adventure was inspirational and, while I wished I could share his attitude, the pain in my bum, the growl in my stomach, and the bugs in my hair just wouldn't allow it.

"Cooper, how can you be so chipper with your legs spread so far over that horse? My rear end is so sore. I think it has disfigured me."

The child extended his legs out to the side and waved his little feet around.

"I'm used to it. I ride Rex every single day. You'll get used to it, too. But for now, a game might keep your mind off it."

Orick rode up next to me and nodded toward Cooper who kept just a few strides in front of us.

"The lad loves games. If ye tell him aye, they'll never end. No as long as he knows ye."

I believed that, but we had little else to keep ourselves occupied on the road. I was willing to try anything that might take my mind off how uncomfortable every bit of me was. I'd been allowed to pack sunscreen, tampons, and a toothbrush, but it seemed that Jane and I both had neglected the necessity of a hair tie and, by this point in our journey, I was almost ready to cut my hair right off.

Angrily, I released the reins of my horse and reached behind me to twist my hair into a knot that would be a tangled mess this evening. I didn't care. I just needed some way to get it off of my neck.

"What sort of game, Cooper? I am in desperate need of a distraction."

"Let's make it a learning game. I'll point out a bird or creature and you tell me what it is. If you know, you tell me about it. If you don't, I'll tell you about it."

I laughed, but I couldn't say *no* after seeing how excited he seemed about it.

"Fine. Who taught you to play games? That hardly sounds like the sort of thing I did when I was a kid. It sounds like school work."

He shrugged, and I hoped I'd not offended him.

"I don't mind things that are like school work since I don't get to go to school. And Mom and my Dad make me play lots of games like this so I keep learning. You ready to play?"

"Absolutely."

Over the course of the afternoon, I learned more about Scottish wildlife and plant growth than I had any need or want to know. Still, it did keep my mind off things like my queasy stomach and painful ass, so it suited me just fine.

I suspected that by mid-afternoon, Orick finally caught on to my grunts and groans and exhales of frustration for he pulled his horse to a stop right at the edge of a beautiful meadow where he said we could rest awhile.

I took full advantage. Within fifteen minutes of dismounting, I conked out on a blanket with Toby tucked into my side.

It was a short rest. When I woke, Cooper slept next to me, and Orick stood by the horses feeding them each a few carrots while he watched them drink from the stream by which we'd tied them.

"How old are you?"

I knew the question was hardly polite, but I'd been wondering about it since the day I met him. When I looked in his eyes, I suspected him to be no more than thirty, but his hands looked a good decade older than that. They were rough and darkened from the sun, and the gait of his walk was that of a man who was accustomed to hard work. Like he had more miles on him than most.

Not to say that there was anything ancient about the way he looked—he wore every year of however old he was remarkably well—so well that even his appearance was enough to make it difficult for me to fathom that he'd lasted this long without getting married. His gorgeous looks combined with how kind and gentle he was and how aware and perceptive he was of those around him, made his single status an oddity I couldn't even wrap my mind around.

"'Tis my thirty-fifth year. Ye must think me verra old."

I meant to laugh but the noise came out as a snort, and I nearly swooned as every ounce of blood rushed to my head in embarrassment. I struggled to recover as I choked out a response and gripped at the tree nearest me for support.

"Hardly. Why aren't you married?"

He smiled and reached over to stroke the side of his horse.

"It seems I've lived many lives, and no a one of them has been my own. I dinna wish to take a wife, to have a family, until I no longer felt indebted to those who saved me."

His answer both intrigued and saddened me.

"Do you mean Adwen? What could you have owed him? You're friends."

A memory must have passed through his mind for a brief sadness seemed to shadow the brilliant blue sparkle in his eyes, but he recovered quickly.

"'Tis a tale for another day but, losing my memory, while it hurts me to know it caused others pain, 'twas a blessing for myself. I now see that I canna wait to start my own life. It helps no one for me to deny myself what others expect for their lives."

I could see then that this was no less of a struggle for him than it was for me. While I kept people at bay so I wouldn't get hurt, he allowed so many in that he worried that his happiness would come at the cost of others. We each had our battles to fight. If he would try, then so would I.

"It's not as easy for you as you make it look, is it? Wanting me—you feel guilty for it?"

He stilled his hand on the horse and looked up as if I said something he'd not thought of before.

"Aye, though I ken now that I canna allow guilt that I shouldna feel to prevent me from having a life of my own."

"I know." I moved close to him and reached my hands upward, placing a hand on either side of his face as I kissed him before pulling back to look into his eyes. "Knowing that you're trying makes me want to try as well. But just know that I'm not good at this stuff. Just ask any ex-boyfriend I've ever had—the endings were my fault. If this doesn't work, just know that it's not your fault. It's mine."

He pulled me into an embrace and rubbed my back as he spoke.

"Why would I think it my fault? Ye'd be a lucky lass to have me."

He swatted my behind, making me jump as he walked away, untying the horses to prepare for us to continue onward. I laughed as I watched him.

I knew he spoke in jest, but every word was true.

Chapter 22

The moment we rode into the village near McMillan Castle, I knew that babies had done little to slow the pace of Grace's family. They beat us by at least a day—the wailing woman in front of the inn was proof of that.

I wondered how long she'd been waiting for Orick to arrive, for I could see how desperate she was to see him. Orick was off his horse and running toward her as soon as he rode up to the inn.

I dismounted more slowly, my bum no more accustomed to sitting atop a horse than it had been three days ago. I stood back and watched Orick scoop the woman up so that her feet lifted off the ground as she sobbed against him.

"Orick, I couldna believe it when Jane told me. To see ye and hold ye, ach ye canna know the joy it brings me."

"It brings me joy to see ye, as well. Ye look as if ye feel much better. There's more health in yer eyes than I've ever seen. I'm so glad of it. Where is Gregor?"

As if summoned, another man walked out the front door of the inn, and Orick lowered Isobel to the ground as he walked over to greet the man.

While Orick spoke to him, Isobel made her way over to introduce herself to me, pulling me into her arms right away.

"Jane spoke of ye, but I doona remember yer name. In truth, I'm too happy to feel bad about it. Do ye mind telling it to me again as I show ye inside for a wee bite to eat and a basin in which ye can clean yerself up from the road?"

I grinned as she released me and took off inside.

"Gladly. My name is Gillian."

"It suits ye. I've laid some things out for ye. 'Twill be far tastier than what ye had on the road. Help yerself to it while I bring the men inside."

She left Cooper, Toby, and me in the dining room. Cooper didn't hesitate to make his way toward the food. It took me all of two seconds to join him.

Isobel couldn't possibly understand just how much better her cooking was compared to what we'd been eating the last three days, and Cooper and I dug in as the rest of them made their way inside.

"I doona want to miss it when Adwen finally sees ye. I hope he hurries home soon. We must make sure we've chairs a plenty near him when he does, for I fear he willna be able to keep on his feet."

Isobel paused long enough to point Orick toward the food but continued as soon as he stepped near it.

"I canna tell ye how the man has grieved for ye. No a day has passed without his mention of ye."

How lucky the two of them were to have such friends. Adwen would be beyond thrilled to see Orick, significantly less so to see me, I imagined. Not after I'd driven him all the way into the village when he clearly needed to leave through the cellar. I wondered how he'd made it back. Had he found another way through, or had I made him walk all the way back to the cellar in the dark, delaying his journey significantly?

I sat there enjoying every bite of food, giving Toby crumbs every few minutes. The pup lay at my feet, mouth open, tongue out as he happily took whatever I would give him.

I enjoyed listening to Orick speak with Gregor and Isobel. The more time I spent around him, the more I could understand why the loss of him had devastated everyone who knew him so completely. He was an excellent conversationalist. He listened and spoke only when his input had value. And nothing he ever said or did was for the show of it.

The afternoon passed by that way, all of us visiting over food and laughter and in comfortable chairs rather than on the back of a horse. Just as evening started in and we readied to go and clean ourselves up, Jane stepped into the inn waving her arms about rather excitedly.

"He's nearly here, he's nearly here. A rider just showed up. He was supposed to let me know that Adwen was headed back, but the rider got delayed so he is just a few moments ahead of him. He should be here by the time the sun goes down. Everybody get over to our house now."

Chapter 23

Within ten minutes, we all stood cramped near the doorway of Adwen and Jane's bedroom in their home. I knew Jane just wanted to talk to Adwen herself before Orick walked out, but it felt as if we were all hiding for a surprise party with each of us straining against the closed door listening for the first sign of Adwen's arrival.

It didn't take long before we heard the voice of the person we waited for.

"Jane, I've missed ye, lass."

Once Adwen spoke, we all backed up a step, as there was no need to crowd against the door. We could hear every word of their exchange easily—Jane's footsteps as she neared him, their embrace followed by a kiss. And then, much to all our awkward dismay, the sound of them moving together and then a thump against one of the walls, as if he'd backed her against it.

Their kissing continued. I looked down at my feet uncomfortably to see Cooper standing in front of me, a finger pointed to the inside of his throat as he made whispered gagging noises.

Eventually, a breathless Jane pulled away, and we all exhaled with relief when she spoke.

"I'm so happy to see you, babe, but this is going to have to wait. I have…" She hesitated. I couldn't imagine how nervous she must be. "Something wonderful has happened that I need to tell you."

"Doona tell me Grace is with child again."

Cooper whirled around in the middle of us and stared at Isobel in question.

She whispered back to him as quietly as she could.

"Doona worry, I doona think she is."

Cooper's face visibly relaxed, and he spun to listen to the rest of the conversation.

Jane laughed in answer to Adwen.

"No. At least…geez I hope she isn't. It's about Orick. I don't know how to tell you this. Will you sit down, Adwen?"

Adwen's voice was deep and stern when he spoke.

"No, Jane. I willna sit."

"He isn't dead."

A noise like a great intake of air that fell somewhere between a growl and a sob traveled through the doorway. My heart squeezed in response to it. Even cold, emotionless me felt something at hearing Adwen's response to the mere mention of the friend he grieved for so much.

"'Tis no kind nor fair of ye to say such a thing. Doona ye know how badly I've wished it? No a day has passed that I have no had to gather every last bit of strength I have to no weep over how I miss him." Adwen's voice broke and his footsteps moved toward the door.

I looked over at Orick and saw him swallow, his eyes brimming with emotion at listening to his friend.

"I canna know why ye said what ye did. I believe I'll see my horse to the stables. I need a moment alone."

"Adwen," Jane called after him, and Orick reached to open the door from inside the bedroom.

"I wouldn't lie to you about something like that. He's here."

At the same moment, Orick pushed the door open and joined Adwen and Jane. The rest of us, determined to not miss a moment of their reunion, crowded into the doorway.

It occurred to me then, watching Adwen's face transform from one of anger and pain to one of pure shock, that this should have been a private moment between them. It would be right for all of us to step away, but I could tell by the riveted faces of those around me that wasn't going to happen.

In truth, it didn't matter whether we were there or not. Adwen didn't see us. The only person he took in was Orick. I expected them to run toward each other, to embrace as Cooper, Jane, and Isobel had all done at seeing him for the first time.

My expectation couldn't have been more off from the reality of what happened.

Instead, Adwen did run toward him, but not with arms open. He ran with his head down and charged Orick's stomach like some sort of really pissed-off bull. Orick fell backward at the impact, sending both men to the floor in a whirlwind of flying fists and feet and grunts of pain.

Both men screamed loudly at the other as they continued rolling around on the floor like animals. Most of what they said was entirely inaudible, but every now and then, one of them would say something that would give the rest of us an idea as to what their conversation was about.

It was absolutely absurd.

"What in the name of Brighid are ye doing in my bedchamber, Orick?"

Orick swung a fist into Adwen's side causing him to spit up on the floor as he groaned.

"Ye are a damned fool. Doona ye wish to know how 'tis that I'm alive before I tell ye why I'm here?"

"No. I can see well enough why ye are no dead. Ye've been tupping my wife, and the two of ye planned this so ye could carry on together whilst I'm away. How could ye do this to me?"

"What the bloody hell are ye talking about, Adwen?"

Orick reached up to block one of Adwen's swings, but Adwen quickly recovered, moving so quickly that he pinned Orick's head between both of his arms. Within moments, Orick started to turn astonishingly red.

Just as I started to worry that Orick would pass out, Jane decided she'd had enough and walked up behind Adwen and stood there about two seconds before rearing back and slapping him so hard across the side of his head that he released Orick on impulse as he whirled around to look at his wife with astonished eyes.

"Ye see fit to hit me after what ye've done?"

Jane crossed her arms and glared at him before she slowly jerked her head over to the rest of us, allowing our presence to do all the talking.

Slowly, both men, now disentangled, pushed themselves to their feet. Once standing, Orick clasped Adwen on the shoulder. They both stared at each other for a long moment and then, in unison, started laughing. The rest of us stared on in disbelief.

"What possessed ye, man? Why would ye say or think such a thing?"

Still laughing at himself and now smiling ear to ear, Adwen stepped back and pointed to Jane.

"Ye walked out of my bedchamber. If ye doona remember, I witnessed Jane kiss ye once before. I know verra well the effect her lips can have on a man."

I looked over to see Jane blush, and the jealousy that rose within me at thinking of the two of them kissing surprised me.

"Ye know she only kissed me to get to ye, ye sodding fool."

Adwen nodded and stifled his laughter as he regarded Orick seriously.

"Aye, but 'twas the only reason for yer absence that came to mind in the moment that I could make any sense of. If ye've been alive, why would ye stay away? It hurts me to think of any reason, for no one of them could be good enough."

Cooper, who apparently had reached his limit of this mess, stepped out from the middle of the doorway and walked straight over in between Adwen and Orick.

"Not so fast, Uncle Adwen. There's definitely one good reason. He didn't remember anything, not until he wandered into the future and saw me. So why don't you just quit being crazy and give him a hug already?"

Adwen looked at Orick in question, the pain in his face easing significantly.

Orick nodded as he reached down to ruffle Cooper's hair.

"Aye, the lad speaks true. For many moons, I dinna ken my own name."

Finally, Adwen's voice broke as emotion overtook him as he moved toward Orick and wrapped his arms around him.

"Why dinna ye say that straight away?"

Orick laughed as they held one another.

"Ye dinna give me a chance before ye knocked my arse to the ground."

"I'm sorry for it. Christ, I'm pleased to see ye."

More love passed between the two of them than I'd ever felt in my life. I had to swallow the lump that rose within me to keep from tearing up at the sight of them. Every time I turned around here, my emotions seemed to surprise me.

Apparently, satisfied that they wouldn't kill each other, Jane did finally decide they needed some time alone and hastily waved all of us from the house and out into the cold.

Cooper laughed as we stepped outside and leaned in to give Jane a hug.

"Well goodnight to you too, Aunt Jane. I'm glad none of us wanted to stay for dinner."

Jane smiled and took off toward Isobel and Gregor's inn with us.

"I think I'll join the rest of you for a little while. Give them a chance to catch up without worrying about filtering in front of a lady."

"Aunt Jane, you're not fooling anybody. You're worse than either one of them. You were born without a filter."

Seemed to me that a lack of filter had been passed down to another little fellow, as well. We all laughed together as Cooper and Jane continued to tease each other as we walked back to Isobel and Gregor's inn together.

Chapter 24

Very late that night, Orick stumbled into the inn as quietly as his heavy feet could manage. He and Adwen would both feel wretched come morning. Neither of them was accustomed to so much ale or so little sleep—years had passed since either of them had indulged in such a way.

Still, while his thoughts seemed to sift through mud and his footsteps came a little less steady, he imagined he could make it to his bedchamber without waking anyone. Until he made it to the staircase and looked up to see Isobel standing at the top, hastily waving him back down into the sitting room.

"Ye will wake Gregor if ye carry on like that. Go and take a seat. I'll light us a candle."

Gregor had a reputation for being unpleasant in his best of moods. Orick certainly didn't wish to wake the man.

It didn't take long for Isobel to join him. Once the room was alight with the flame of a small candle, she pulled him aside.

"I dinna know if ye'd come back at all this evening. When Jane left to go back home and ye dinna return, I thought ye might stay there."

"Ach," Orick threw his arms up and marveled at how loosely they seemed to move around him. "Well, the thought did occur to me, but Adwen wouldna allow it. Said that no matter how pleased he was to see me, he was more eager to take his wife to bed, most especially after she joined us in a few cups of ale and became rather jolly herself."

Isobel shook her head, but Orick could tell it was not so much in disapproval but amusement.

"I'm sure she did. I'd wager the lass can outdrink ye both."

"Aye, she can. I dinna mean to wake ye, Isobel. Ye should be asleep."

Isobel guided him to a chair and sat down next to him.

"Ye dinna wake me. I slept for awhile and then woke to relieve myself when I noticed the candles still burning in Gillian's room. I decided to wait for yer return so I could advise ye to no be a fool."

Orick waited for Isobel to explain.

"She's a lovely lass."

The loveliest he'd ever seen.

"Aye, she is."

"And ye wish for her to be yers, aye?"

"Aye."

"Then ye must behave like it. Now, any lad could see her and no ken that ye fancy her. Ye dinna touch her, and ye hardly said a word to her since ye arrived. She likes ye, though a lass needs to ken that she is fancied in return, or she canna open her heart. She needs to ken that ye like her."

Orick hoped Gillian didn't doubt his interest. He thought about her every moment.

"I've told her that I fancy her. 'Tis why she's here."

"Telling and showing are two verra different things, and ye men folk are no so talented at realizing that. She stays awake hoping ye'll come to her. Doona disappoint the lass. 'Tis why I stayed awake—to keep ye from the fool mistake that most men would make."

Orick stood and had to reach for the wall to steady himself. His vision was clearing quickly, but the sudden movement threw him.

"I doona think it best tonight. Do ye no see my flushed cheeks and red eyes? I'm more into the drink than I've a right to be, and I'm so tired that I canna think well enough. I wouldna know what to say to her. No to mention that I still carry the filth from the road. I worry if I see the lass tonight, I willna behave like a gentleman."

Isobel smiled and gripped his arm as they walked up the stairs together.

"She willna care if yer dirty. She's no had the chance to clean up herself. Ye know, I was once a young lass myself, and I ken from my own experience—there is no much that lassies fancy more than a true gentleman who, on verra special occasions, forgets that he's one. No lassie wants a perfect man, and ye come as close to being one as any man can, Orick. Show her that at times ye can be as weak as any man, and she'll love ye more for it."

"Do ye no think it improper for me to go to her bedchamber in the middle of the night?"

Isobel smiled and brought them to a halt as they neared Gillian's door.

"Aye, verra improper. Now get yerself inside."

Isobel gave him little choice, reaching up to knock on the door before scurrying inside her own room.

Chapter 25

My eyes ached from straining to see in the light of the candle, but I enjoyed working so much that I didn't care. I always found it difficult to go even a day without painting. To go three had me ready to pull out my hair. Luckily, I found relief in a small art pad and a few pieces of charcoal Jane allowed me to pack, and I took them out to sketch after we made it back from Jane and Adwen's house. Before I knew it, hours upon hours had gotten away from me.

Not that I would've been able to sleep even if I hadn't busied myself drawing. I was so tired and sore from riding that I was in that semi-delirious state where you're too tired to even sleep. I thought I might as well do something with my time rather than lay there looking up at the ceiling.

When I first heard knuckles against the door, I worried for a moment that it was already daylight. Then I looked over to the window to see the moon still hanging high, and I thought at once it must be Cooper. The kid was a serious insomniac, and he never seemed to hesitate at all to barge into somebody's bedroom. I was honestly surprised that he even knocked.

Toby was up in an instant as he leapt off the bed and ran to the door, tail wagging, eager to see his new little buddy. I stood more slowly and reached for a rag to clean my charcoal-covered hands, stretching before moving to crack open the door.

When I saw Orick rather than Cooper standing outside, I nearly shut the door in his face in response to the nerves that fluttered inside me. Toby prevented me from doing that as he clawed at Orick's legs until he bent down to pick him up.

I looked at him and waved him inside, quickly shutting the door so our conversation wouldn't disturb anyone else.

"Orick, what are you doing here? I figured you would stay over at Adwen's tonight."

He held Toby close and allowed the pup to lick all over his face before he moved across the room and set the dog down on the bed.

"I saw the candlelight from beneath yer door and thought ye might be awake."

I noticed that he stood a bit awkwardly in the middle of the room, oddly stiff in his posture. He spoke very deliberately, very slowly. I thought perhaps he was nervous, which helped to alleviate my own anxiety considerably. I decided to step toward him and rest a hand on his arm to soothe him. Once I was closer, I could smell the liquor distinctly enough that I knew it went a long way toward accounting for his strange behavior.

"Yes, I am. I've just been drawing." I pointed over to the sketchpad and watched him look at it before he nodded and smiled uncomfortably.

"Ach, ye were drawing. No waiting. I'm sorry to have disturbed ye, lass."

He tried to step toward the door, but I moved over to block his way.

"Waiting? What are you talking about?"

"'Tis nothing. Isobel said," he hesitated and reached up to run a hand through his hair. "It doesna matter what she said. I'll speak of it with her come morning. I best leave ye."

I enjoyed seeing him like this, uncertain, uncomfortable, and trying his hardest to hide the fact that he was quite drunk. He did a very bad job.

"Nope. It's not nothing. Isobel sent you into my room at two in the morning? Why would she do that?"

He tried to sidestep me, and I reached out to grab his arm. It only succeeded in pulling him in closer to me.

"Do ye mean to embarrass me, lass? I'm already that. She thought ye stayed awake to wait for me. I see now that she was wrong."

"Oh. I'm sorry. I wasn't. I just got caught up in drawing, but why would you be embarrassed?" I didn't move where from I stood. Whether it was purposeful or if it was only the result of his unsteady feet I didn't know, but he took another step toward me.

"I ken ye can tell well enough, Gillian. I am no a man accustomed to so much drink. 'Tis Adwen's doing. I should be looking in yer eyes. Instead I canna pull my gaze away from the round tips of yer nipples showing through yer nightgown. It embarrasses me to no be so in control of my thoughts. Ye should let me bid ye goodnight."

I blushed and took a quick glance downward at the thin gown Isobel had given to me. I'd thought little of it when I opened the door, but Orick was right, my breasts were astonishingly visible. I crossed my arms self-consciously, but my heart sped up and my chest started to rise and fall in quick succession at his words. I hadn't noticed him staring at my breasts. As tall as he was, I always felt like I stared at his chin anyway.

I let loose a soft laugh in an attempt to lighten the mood, though it came out breathless and rather needy, and I didn't miss how his breath caught in his throat at the sound of it.

"Even if Isobel thought I was waiting on you, why did she send you up here?"

Now that he'd confessed it, his eyes, though he did make eye contact, repeatedly kept dropping downward. I took a step closer to him just to keep him from doing so. When I did, his breath became shaky and, hesitantly, he moved a hand and rested it on the side of my hip.

"She said that I dinna treat ye well today. That if I mean to capture yer heart, I must do more than tell ye I care for ye. I must show ye as well, and I dinna do that today. I wouldna want ye to feel neglected."

Today was exhausting for everyone. I'd not thought a thing about his behavior toward me.

The feeling of his light grip on my waist made me tremble. I now stood so close to him that with every breath, my nipples dragged up and down his chest. I could hear his shaky intake of breath, and I knew it took all his strength to keep his hand from traveling elsewhere.

I looked up at him and said his name so that he'd look into my eyes. When he did so, shockwaves shot through my whole body.

"I didn't feel neglected, not at all. Today was about you and Adwen, as it should have been, but Isobel was right about one thing." I reached a hand up to gently brush my thumb across his cheek. "Sometimes it is nice to be shown just exactly how a man feels."

That was all it took for his mouth to sink down, consuming my neck and lips as he cupped at my breast and moved his other hand to my backside. I relaxed against him, allowing him to feel and touch me over the fabric of my nightgown, and I moaned as his teeth grazed against my earlobe.

He shook with need, and I wrapped my legs around him as he lifted me and carried me over to the bed. He lay me down and followed me downward, rolling onto his side next to me as he kissed me once more, slipping his hand underneath the gown to feel my bare skin. He cupped his hand in between my legs, and we both groaned at the sensation of it. I shrugged out of the loose neck of the gown, pushing my breasts out the top, exposing them to the air for a brief moment as he pulled one of my nipples deep into his mouth.

I cried out and wove my hands into his hair, pulling it so that he moaned as I gently scratched my fingernails against the back of his neck.

Toby jumped off the bed understanding that his presence intruded on something too personal for him to be in the middle of.

Everything was an exquisite sensation. We touched and fondled and grasped at one another with a need so raw that neither of us could breathe. Eventually, he rolled on top of me, spreading my legs with his knee as he gathered the bottom of my gown with his hands, pushing it upwards so that he could touch me.

I reached down to him in kind. As I stroked him, he stilled his body as if my hand on him woke him up from his blind need.

He stopped and collapsed his forehead against my own, kissing me gently as he struggled to catch his breath. Slowly, he rolled to his side and pulled me against his chest.

"I'm sorry, lass, but I canna have ye, no like this. No when I'm no myself."

I understood and respected him for it, no matter how desperately I wanted to be with him.

"Okay." I nodded against him, and we lay together both catching our breath as we tried to subdue our need for one another.

After a time, neither of us shook quite as badly. I turned and smiled up at him.

"Do you want to talk instead?"

He grinned and bent his head to kiss me. My whole body lit afire for him once more.

"'Tis naught to do with ye, lass, but I doona think I can talk anymore this night."

"Did you and Adwen talk each other's ears off?"

He reached to brush the hair from my face.

"Aye. Might I simply hold ye instead, Gillian? Lay here and watch ye fall asleep?"

Nothing sounded better, but I looked down to see Toby sitting by the bed on the floor, just waiting for my permission.

"Yes, I don't want to move from your arms. As long as you don't mind sharing the bed with a dog, because you're sort of in Toby's spot."

He laughed and patted the small empty space next to us, and Toby jumped right up in response.

"No, o'course I doona. I wouldna dare take the wee pup's place. He's more deserving of a soft bed than most humans."

I couldn't agree with him more. As I snuggled in against his chest, I tried to ignore the small voice in the back of my mind that said I had fallen in love with Orick right then and there. The icy fortress around my heart was melting fast.

Chapter 26

Morning came much too quickly. When I woke, still in Orick's arms, I found him wide awake, looking down at me with a happy smile that warmed me all over.

"Tell me you slept some."

He nodded and squeezed me in close with the arm he had wrapped around me.

"Aye, though ye snore something fierce."

I sat up rather defensively, shrugging my shoulders back into my gown, horrified at his claim.

"I do not." Although, in truth, I had no way to really know since I wasn't accustomed to sharing my bed with another.

"Aye, ye do." He laughed and, now that he was no longer pinned to the bed by my body, he stood and stretched.

"That's mortifying."

"Ach, doona worry yerself over it. I've spent years on the road with men who snore so loud the horses canna sleep. It dinna bother me."

He made his way over to the door, and I stood to follow him.

"Well, let's just not ever mention that again, okay?"

He bent to kiss me as he reached for the handle.

"Aye, I willna do so again. 'Tis time I make my way to my room so no one knows I stayed here. 'Twould shame ye if someone saw me leave here."

The thought didn't worry me whatsoever.

"Who cares? We didn't even do anything."

"I care, lass. I willna have ye dishonored on my account. Besides, I'm so covered in road dirt, I'll have to bathe 'til midday to clean myself."

He started to open the door, and I suddenly remembered something I meant to ask him hours ago.

"Hang on. What did Adwen learn about his dad and brother? Are they okay?"

Orick's face twisted into a frustrated expression of disgust. I could tell right away that at the very least, no harm had come to them. He shut the door as he turned to answer me.

"Aye, they're fine enough though I doona expect either Lennox or Griffith are pleased to be spending their days in captivity."

"Captivity?" Perhaps seventeenth century folk defined *fine enough* differently than I did.

"Aye and they deserve to be there. The fools gambled their way into a grave debt with Laird Macaslan. When they couldna pay it, he arrested them on the road and took them for safekeeping at his castle until the debt is paid. Adwen is on his way to talk to Baodan, laird of McMillan Castle, as we speak to see if he can borrow what is needed for their release."

"Will he give it to them?"

"Aye. He will." Orick fidgeted in the doorway. I could tell he wanted to say something more.

"What is it?"

"I told Adwen I would go back with him to Macaslan Castle. Callum stayed there as the laird's guest. Jane will come so ye are welcome to join us, though since ye are no married, 'twill have to be under the pretense that ye are Jane's lady maid. Laird Maccaslan is no a forward-thinking man. 'Tis the only way he will approve of ye traveling with us. Ye should also know that the journey is likely to last the month. I know ye told Aiden and Anne that ye would be gone no more than a fortnight."

I knew Aiden and Anne both well enough to know that they wouldn't worry if I didn't show up when expected. They would just assume I got carried away with everything. I didn't want to go back. Not now, when I felt like we were just starting to get to really know one another. For once, I felt like it might be possible for me to share normal human emotions with another person.

"Is there a way I could get word to Aiden and Anne?"

"Aye, Jane often sends messages back somehow. Seek her help in the matter."

"Great." I reached around him and opened the door to my room, eager to get myself cleaned up as well. "Now go get into that tub you've been talking about. You're kind of smelly."

Chapter 27

Come that afternoon, I found myself standing face to face with my only true nemesis here in the seventeenth century—my broad-backed horse named Grock. My legs, hips, and ass hurt just looking at him.

"Are you sure we can't just hook some sort of wagon up to him, and he can pull me the whole way there? He looks strong enough, I think."

Adwen, who stood closest to me tying packs to the back of each horse, laughed and shook his head apologetically. Orick was inside the inn gathering a few days' worth of food that Isobel had somehow miraculously whipped up this morning.

"I'm sorry, lass, but no. We will travel down some steep roads and small trails. Even if we had such a thing, 'twould no be possible. Ye will grow accustomed to it with time."

"Yeah. That's what everybody keeps saying, but I really don't think so."

Grock blew air through his lips as if he were laughing at me.

With Grock all packed up with the few belongings I had, I reached for Toby's cloth sling and draped it over my head. The moment the pup saw me slip it on and looked around at the horses, he put two and two together and started whining pathetically.

"I know. Trust me you're going to have a better time with it than I will. At least you get to ride comfortably."

I picked Toby up, and he continued to whine as I carried him around in an effort to avoid climbing aboard the horse until I absolutely had to. I turned at the sound of hooves approaching and watched Cooper proudly gallop toward us on his miniature horse.

Toby started to squirm out of my arms and wag his tail frantically the moment he saw Cooper. As soon as Cooper pulled on his reins and dismounted, Toby flew out of my arms and charged toward him, jumping into the child's open arms to lick his face repeatedly.

Cooper took to sitting on the ground with the pup, giggling and stroking Toby as he bobbed and weaved his head to try and avoid the brunt of the dog's kisses. There was really no escaping them.

I watched the two of them together and, reluctantly, made a rather obvious decision. Taking the sling off, I rolled it up and carried it over to Cooper.

"I have a big favor to ask of you, kiddo."

Cooper spotted the sling right away.

"Don't tell me you are going to leave Toby here? Oh, Gillian that would be so awesome. I would take such good care of him, I promise. I would play with him and make sure Isobel doesn't feed him too much bread, and I will clean him up when he gets dirty."

I feared that if I didn't interrupt, the child would go on forever. I reached out a hand and touched his knee gently.

"Yes, I've decided I'm going to leave Toby in your care if you're okay with that. But you've got to keep him with you all of the time, okay? And take care of him like he was your very own?"

He bent down and kissed Toby right on the side of his face.

"I will. I'll even let him sleep in my bed with me."

I laughed and reached to take Toby from him so I could squeeze him goodbye.

"You just read my mind. That's what I was about to ask you next."

"Trust me, Gillian. You couldn't leave him in better hands. You won't have to worry about him at all while you're gone."

Toby allowed me to scratch his head briefly but then wiggled out of my arms and back into Cooper's.

"I know I won't. I appreciate you doing this."

Cooper smiled, and we both turned our heads as Adwen spoke to us from the front of the inn.

"Time to leave, lass. Cooper, come bid me and yer Aunt Jane goodbye."

Within just a few short hours of leaving, I felt like Jane was an old girlfriend. Having her on the road with us did wonders to keep me from thinking on the state of my rear end overmuch. I found her to be wickedly funny and forward with everything she said. Her blunt tongue seemed to put both Adwen and Orick at ease, and I found that we all seemed to talk rather freely with one another, laughing and chatting about a million random things.

During one of our necessary bathroom stops, I took the opportunity to speak with Adwen about something that had been bothering me for days.

"I'm sorry for being so difficult with you during your last day at Cagair Castle."

He didn't quite turn completely to look at me, but I saw the corner of his mouth turn up in a smile.

"Doona be sorry, lass. Ye dinna know the truth then, and I know we did plenty that seemed strange to ye."

"Yes, but I still hate that I drove you all the way to the village when you didn't need to go there. How did you get back to the castle?"

He did turn toward me then and stared at me plainly.

"I waited for ye to no be able to see me, and I walked back in the rain."

I looked down at the ground in an amused apology.

"Yeah…I figured that. I really am sorry."

Just then, Orick and Jane reappeared from the wide expanse of trees where they'd each gone in search of a private place to relieve themselves.

"Sorry for what?" Jane mounted her horse with ease, and I wondered how long it would take me to be able to do the same.

"For insisting that I drive him to the village."

She laughed and looked back over her shoulder at me.

"It didn't hurt him. It's not that far of a walk. We all found it rather amusing."

Adwen glared teasingly at his wife and mounted his horse.

"Aye, well it doesna surprise me that ye took pleasure from it. Ye have a strange sense of humor."

Jane laughed, and reluctantly I allowed Orick to help me back atop Grock. He surprised me by giving me a quick, soft kiss on the cheek before pushing me upward.

"Thank you."

"Yer welcome. Just a wee bit further, and we shall reach our resting place for the night. If 'twas only Adwen and I, we would sleep under the stars, but we ken ye and Jane wouldna enjoy it. 'Tis a small inn with only two rooms. Will ye pretend, just for a night, that ye are my wife? If ye doona wish it, I'll make camp out here with the horses, and I willna mind doing so. I'd understand."

I smiled and started nodding before he finished.

"That means that we get to share a room, yes?"

Orick stood next to Grock with one hand on the horse's neck and the other on my thigh. He gave me a light squeeze as he answered.

"Aye."

I smiled and leaned down to kiss him, fully aware that Adwen and Jane watched our every move. When I pulled away, I winked at him.

"Then, aye, husband. Lead us to the inn."

Chapter 28

From the outside, the inn looked like it was barely large enough to hold a room for the owner, let alone an additional two for guests. The rooms had to be the size of closets and the beds not much larger than a crib. Still, no matter how small the rooms or the beds, I would find it preferable to sleeping outside, so I said nothing as we stopped in front of the place.

"Fionn is no back from his hunt. Ye must stay outside until he is."

Adwen dismounted with an aggravated groan and went to go talk to the old woman who stood in the doorway. She greeted us with her arms crossed tightly against her chest, her blatant frown a stark difference from Isobel's ecstatic welcome.

"Shona, ye ken well enough who I am. Ye ken Orick, as well. Do ye no trust that we willna steal from ye nor harm ye?

Shona took a step toward Adwen as he approached and shooed the group of us away.

"Aye, I ken ye Adwen MacChristy. Last time ye stayed here, ye had that one," she pointed at Orick, "sneak in Willy's daughter for an after dinner tup. The man still willna speak to me for allowing such things to happen in my home. If ye wish to stay here, the group of ye will wait in the stables for Fionn. The choice will be his."

Adwen laughed and reached for his horse's reins as he led us to the stables.

"Aye, fine, we shall wait, but ye know Fionn will grant us entry."

The woman huffed and turned to go back inside.

Jane glared at Adwen the entire way back to the stables, waiting until we were completely inside to say a word.

"You really used to be a tool, didn't you?"

Adwen laughed as he patted his horse affectionately. Orick spoke up in affirmation.

"I doona ken what ye mean by *tool*, but aye, he was a wretch."

Jane whirled on him and quickly put Orick in his place as well.

"Like you're that much better, seeing as you snuck them in and out of the place."

Orick looked down at his feet as he dismounted, and I ran my hand through his hair playfully as he came to help me off of my horse. I could tell she'd been successful at embarrassing him.

Once I was off my horse, I reached to the small packsack where Isobel had placed our food and hurried to try to change the conversation.

"Anybody hungry? Why don't we eat something while we wait for permission to go inside?"

I didn't wait for anyone to answer as I plopped myself down and yanked out a piece of dried meat and dug in. Slowly, the rest of them joined me.

Orick leaned over as we ate.

"Thank ye for that. I feared Adwen was about to start sharing stories about me that I'd rather ye no hear just yet."

I smiled and reached for the bread, speaking to him with my mouth full.

"We're each entitled to our secrets, I suppose. We can share them in our own time."

"Aye, we can." Orick stood and extended a hand to help me do the same. "Fionn approaches."

I couldn't hear anything that would make him think that.

"How do you know?"

"I canna hear him yet if 'tis what ye wondered. I just saw him pass through the trees behind ye."

"Oh." I grasped at his hand and stood up.

Adwen quickly did the same. While Jane and I gathered up the food, the men went to go and greet him. Fionn seemed to know them right away and called out to them as soon as he was close enough to tell who they were.

"Adwen, Orick, has Shona no let ye in? I canna say it surprises me. She doesna care for the two of ye at all. She does no have a pleasant way about her to begin with, and mention of either of ye brings out the worst in her. Still, I'm happy to see ye both. Do tie up yer horses and follow me in."

Fionn swung off the back of his horse with the energy of a man half his age before happily clasping both Adwen and Orick on the shoulder. Jane did the same to me in jest as we all walked toward Fionn's home together.

"Are ye well, Fionn?" Orick asked as the three of them walked in step together.

"Aye, well enough, though I came across a troublesome sight far into the forest yesterday morn. I havena been able to keep my mind off it since."

"What did ye see?" Orick pulled away from the odd little train as they neared the front of the house. They couldn't all fit through the door standing next to one another.

"I offered help to a lass who needed it badly. She wouldna take it, and I ken she will die without it. More than that, she wouldna let me near her. She held a spear. I doona doubt she would have thrown it had I tried to get closer to her than I was."

Orick's steps stopped immediately at Fionn's words, but he didn't say a word as Adwen spoke.

"Was the lass alone? What happened to her?"

"I doona ken what happened to the lass. She wouldna say a word to me other than I best get going unless I wished to die with her. She was all alone and accustomed to being so. Her side was near split open, whether it be man or animal that caused her wound, I canna ken for sure."

Jane and I stood back, both of us taking notice of the tension in Orick's stance. He reached out to grasp Fionn's shoulder.

"What did the lass look like? Describe her to me."

Fionn turned, concern etched in his face at Orick's panicked interest.

"She has skin darkened from the sun and hair even darker. I doona think she lives an easy life. She dinna trust me, no matter how I tried to help her."

I knew who it was. Orick had mentioned her name often during the short time I'd known him.

"'Tis Marion. I must go to her."

Chapter 29

Orick didn't delay his goodbye; he kept it short and to the point before he took off in the middle of the darkness in search of Marion. Adwen tried to leave with him, but Orick wouldn't allow it, stating as firmly as I'd ever seen him do anything that Marion wouldn't want anyone other than him to get near her.

He wished for the rest of us to continue our journey to Macaslan Castle. He would meet us there just as soon as he could. Without him there, my presence on the trip seemed more than a little out of place. Still, Jane and Adwen were nothing but kind and inclusive of me as we traveled the next day, making sure to keep their hands off one another, only having conversations that I could carry on with them.

I appreciated their effort to include me, but I couldn't stop thinking about Orick. In that brief moment before he left after Marion, I saw more concern, thought, and emotion from him than I'd felt in myself in the last decade. What did that say about me? A good many things, I imagined, the most obvious being that I was a terrible match for a man so selfless as Orick.

I knew the woman Fionn spoke of was most likely Marion the moment I saw Orick stop walking toward the house. Of course he would go to her. I wouldn't expect anything less. It seemed rather obvious to me, and it didn't bother me in the slightest.

She was injured and very possibly dying—even a man lacking the profound moral compass Orick lived by would have gone to try and help her. What amazed me was that even in that moment, where I was certain all I would have been able to think about was my concern over my friend, he kept thinking about everyone else.

He worried about leaving Adwen to deal with Laird Macaslan on his own, and he felt guilty about leaving me when he was the one who invited me along. I just about had to shake it into him that I understood.

"I'll make it up to ye, Gillian. Ye canna know how much I hate to leave ye. I owe Marion a great debt, and I canna leave her out there if she's hurt."

He had nothing he needed to make up to me. Had it been my friend, I wouldn't think twice, wouldn't worry for a moment about anyone else that I left behind while leaving to help them—Orick cared about others almost too much.

He felt that he needed to be everything to everyone. The thing was, he had enough love and strength within him to be that. Most of the time, I felt like I didn't even have enough of all that good stuff inside me to give it to myself, let alone someone else. He deserved someone with a heart like his.

"He will be okay, you know? I'm now convinced more than ever that Orick's part cat. He has nine lives or something."

I glanced over at Jane who was watching me closely.

"I know. I'm not worried about him. I was thinking about myself actually. Isn't that terrible? I should be worried about him and instead I'm riding along thinking about how much better off he would be without me. I don't think about others the same way he does. I don't care about anything the way he cares about strangers he meets. He needs to be with someone like him."

Jane twisted her face up in disapproval.

"Why would you think that? Can you imagine if he was with someone just like him? Someone who did worry and think about everyone else all the time? They would nauseate each other. It would just be too much of everything in one place. Opposites attract for a reason. You're not supposed to be the same. Perhaps there are areas where he is weak and you are strong and vice versa. As long as you love each other, that's what counts. Quit thinking about it so much. You're trying to make it hard on yourself, trying to think of reasons to end it and move on so that you don't get hurt."

I knew that was part of it. I did it with every relationship I'd ever been in.

She reached between us and squeezed my knee as if she knew she was right.

"That won't work with Orick. He doesn't let people give up, so quit fighting with yourself and just enjoy the ride. Besides," she paused and pointed off into the distance to the large expanse of stone we were riding towards, "you'd be better off preparing yourself for the unpleasant event that lies ahead. Laird Macaslan is a total ass, and Adwen's changed his mind about the story. You're no longer my maid, you're my cousin—that way you'll get to stay in a decent room and be allowed to eat dinner with us. Just remember that we're not in the twenty-first century anymore. He has to think that you're my cousin so don't say anything no matter how ridiculous the man is. If we want to help Adwen get Lennox and Griffith released, we will have to play his game."

Chapter 30

Marion traveled a distance far greater than Orick would have expected since last he'd seen her. It made him wonder more than once as he traveled through the night if the lass he sought was indeed Marion. But then he would think of Fionn's description and the spear she'd wielded at him, and he knew it could be none other than her. He only hoped he wouldn't be too late and that when he found her, she would allow him to help.

She was the most stubborn lass he'd ever known, and he was accustomed to being around his share of strong-willed women. If she refused his help as she had done Fionn's, there was little he could do about it.

Despite his worry, he moved through the forest at a slow pace. He couldn't overtire his horse who had already put in a full day's work. Besides that, it was so difficult to see that he wanted to make sure he didn't pass any signs of her in the darkness.

It helped that he knew her patterns, knew from staying with her for so long the sort of place she would dwell in. It would be near the water, whether a stream or the ocean. Marion wanted to hear the sound of water moving across the earth. That, at least, allowed him to narrow his search significantly. He found the stream that ran through the forest and followed along its bank, watching for any unusual covering or caves where Marion might have holed up.

He searched all night. When the sun started to peak over the horizon, his heart felt like lead inside him. If Fionn thought her near death the day before, how did he expect to find anything more than her lifeless body now? He shook his head and pulled his horse to a stop, climbing down to walk to the edge of the river where he dipped his face down into the cool water.

It wouldn't do for him to think that way, not until he knew for sure what had happened to her and where she was. Fatigue had the ability to turn even the most level-headed man mad. He couldn't allow his own sleepiness to poison the hope he held for her.

He pulled his face from the water, allowing the droplets from his face to drip down his neck and beneath his shirt as he closed his eyes and breathed in deep, silently praying for the safety of his friend and the strength he needed to keep going until he found her.

A loud clap caused him to jerk and look up from where he sat hunched over the water on his knees. He turned in the direction of the noise to see a fawn darting away from an opening in the grass—a small hill with an opening, an opening covered by foliage until the fawn dared to near it.

It was just the sort of den where Marion would seek refuge. If she were badly injured, it would be an easy enough place to pull herself inside. Orick stood, tied his horse to a nearby tree, and pulled off his sack full of food before approaching slowly. Whatever her state, Marion could fend away the most unruly intruder. He didn't wish to end up on the receiving end of her fishing spear.

"Marion," he called out to her as he approached, hoping if she knew it was him, she would call for him.

When no response came from inside the small underbrush, he reached down to lift the foliage away with his arm. He saw her right away, lying on her side with her back against the inside of the small space, her eyes closed.

Sadness pulled at him, but as he reached inside to touch her, he pulled back at the warmth of her skin. She wasn't dead, not yet anyway, and he quickly lay on his own side so that he could push his way in next to her.

She breathed, but her breaths came sporadically, each one a little weaker than the last. He could see no proof of injury, at least not right away. But as the sun rose higher and shined light onto them, his eyes caught sight of the sticky pool beneath her and the wide-open gash in her side. She had the wound pressed tightly against the ground. He could see then that she lay on her side for that purpose, to keep from bleeding as best she could.

He shook her gently, whispering her name and hoping with his every word that she would wake up in time to see him, that she would die knowing that she wasn't alone. And die, she would. There was no potion nor stitch that would heal Marion's injuries. They were too vast and had sat too long. A fever raged within her. He could feel its heat without touching her. He'd only just made it in time.

"Marion, Marion, wake up, lass. 'Tis Craig." The name seemed much less uncomfortable to him now that he knew his real name. Now it seemed a reminder of the affection he and Marion had for one another.

Slowly, on a great intake of breath that caused blood to pool on the stained dirt beneath, she opened her eyes, taking a moment to register him before she smiled.

"Have I died, or is it truly ye, Craig? I dinna think I would see ye again in this life."

Orick gathered Marion's limp hands into his own and brought them to his mouth as he kissed them.

"Ye havena died yet. I'm here. I shall stay here with ye until the end."

Marion chuckled just once before closing her eyes at the effort. Orick moved in closer and allowed her head to rest against his shoulder as he gathered her to him.

"Thank ye for no lying to me—for no saying I wouldna die."

For some, such blunt words would have been inappropriate, but Orick knew that Marion would appreciate nothing less than the truth.

"Ye ken well enough the extent of yer injuries, Marion. What happened to ye?"

"'Twas foolish and my own doing. I pushed my spear into the ground whilst I climbed a tree to see where I was. I stepped on a rotten branch and fell from high onto my spear."

"Marion." Orick glanced down at the wound once more. He could scarcely believe it hadn't killed her at once. "And ye pulled it out on yer own?"

"Aye. I couldna leave it in me, and I dinna see a choice. 'Twas early yesterday morn."

"I'm sorry that I was no…"

She hushed him. "No. Doona be sorry for anything. Tell me. I can see ye remember, for ye've changed."

Orick smiled and reached to brush the hair from Marion's eyes.

"Aye. I remember. I told ye my name was no Craig. 'Tis Orick."

Marion's eyes changed at his words, and she lifted her head as much as she could.

"What did ye say?"

"My real name is Orick, but ye can call me Craig, Marion. I doona mind it."

Marion closed her eyes and pulled her hands free of him, gently resting one of them on his chest as she took a strangled breath to gather her strength.

"No wonder I felt I could trust ye, to help ye when ye fell from that cliff and washed ashore at my feet. Do ye think ye can carry me, Orick?"

Orick shifted and lifted himself to an elbow, surprised at both her request and her use of his real name. If he lifted her from the ground, she would die in a matter of minutes.

"Aye. I can lift ye, but do ye truly wish me to? Ye know ye will go quickly if I do."

Marion nodded.

"Do ye no ken where we are, Orick? I traveled this way so I could see the place I grew up. Allow me to see it before I die. And when I go, I want ye to bury me near it."

He didn't know where they were, not exactly, though the forest did feel familiar to him.

"Wrap yer arms around me as best ye can. I will have to slide ye out before I can lift ye. 'Twill cause ye pain."

"The pain willna last long. Ye will wish to see what I do. Hurry."

He did as she asked, sliding from beneath the small shelter and pulling her toward him before lifting her easily into his arms. She pointed in the direction she meant for him to go, and he climbed the short hill, every ounce of breath leaving him as he reached the top.

From the top of the hill looking downward, all he could see was an open expanse of grass forever burned into his mind. He knew right away why Marion had lived the secluded life she had. He'd grown dangerously close to living the same sort of life once himself. For the land they both looked down on led straight to his family home. The structure itself was long since gone, set on fire by his own hands after finding his parents murdered.

He looked down at Marion with wide, tear-filled eyes as he watched her breathing slow.

"Is yer name truly *Marion*?"

Marion turned her head toward the clearing, and Orick bent to kiss her forehead as she answered him with her last breath.

"No little brother, 'tis Maidie."

He slumped to the ground as she died. Orick held his sister close as he wept for her.

Chapter 31

While the laird's greeting was friendly enough, his phony charade quickly disappeared by nightfall when we all gathered for dinner.

Laird Macaslan sat at the head of the table and quickly directed his eldest son and his wife to sit to his left. Following the assumption that the left side of the table was for the married couples, Adwen and Jane filed in beside them, leaving me, Callum, and the laird's youngest son, Drostan, to figure out our own seating on the opposite side of the table.

Unconsciously, I gravitated toward the middle but was quickly ushered to the end farthest from the laird by Callum's guiding hand. It was the first interaction I'd ever had with Adwen's brother, and I appreciated his guidance immensely.

"Best ye sit on this side of me. The laird has wandering eyes, and his son a wandering hand. I doona wish to see ye groped over yer stew." I smiled and nodded in appreciation as I took my seat.

"Laird Macaslan, thank ye for the meal and for the hospitality ye've show me while Adwen was gone in search of what's owed ye. I offer my apologies for the debt my Da and Griffith acquired. Adwen has gathered what ye are owed. I hope that this unfortunate incident willna affect relations between our clans."

It surprised me for a moment to hear Callum address the laird, as Adwen was the eldest. But then I remembered Adwen and Jane's quaint little home in McMillan territory and the brief mention that Adwen had released his title to Callum.

The position seemed to suit him. He spoke with confidence, and there was an authority in the tone of his voice I could tell Laird Macaslan didn't appreciate.

The old man stared at Callum, taking a long moment to take a swig of his ale before plastering a phony smile on his face.

"I canna see why it would. Ye brought what was owed to me."

Callum nodded and tipped his glass in the laird's direction.

"Good. Then we shall enjoy this meal together, and ye will release my brother and Da so that we may all be on our way come morning."

"No." Laird Macaslan slammed his fist down on the table as he spoke.

Movement from across the table caught my eye, and I looked over to see Adwen reaching beneath the table to squeeze Jane's leg in warning. She visibly twitched with anger at the laird's response to Callum, and I wondered then why Jane felt the need to tell me not to speak to the laird. Clearly, she was going to have a much more difficult time keeping her mouth shut than I was.

Callum kept his voice level as he spoke, but I could see the tension in his jaw as I sat next to him. "I'm sorry. I doona ken yer meaning. The debt owed to ye is paid. Ye will release them." The laird's expression changed once more back to one of strained friendliness. He was as changeable as the wind, and I found being around him to be rather exhausting.

"Aye, o'course. I only meant that I willna discuss such matters over dinner."

The muscles on either side of Callum's jaw bulged out as he refrained from saying anything further. Instead, he simply nodded and bent to shovel food into his mouth.

The laird quickly followed suit and changed the conversation to something about hunting. While he spoke to Adwen about it, Callum turned to speak to me.

"I'm pleased to meet ye, Gillian. Adwen spoke of ye when he arrived, though I dinna think ye'd be following the rest of them through. I'm glad ye did. Orick's needed a match for a long time. Ach, I canna believe he's alive. I canna wait to see him."

"He will be happy to see you, I'm sure. He's a bit of a blowhard, isn't he?"

I nodded my head toward Macaslan, and Callum nearly spit up stew at the expression.

"Ye speak just as Jane does. Aye, the man is a fool and an arse, and it pains me that we are under his control here. I doona feel things will go as easily as they should. He is no the sort of man to keep his end of a bargain."

As if Callum's words summoned trouble, Laird Macaslan spoke up loudly from the end of the table. I could scarcely breathe when I realized the question was directed at me.

"Yer husband must be a fool to allow ye to visit yer cousin without him. Why is he no with ye?"

I responded instinctively before I had a chance to remember Jane's advice.

"I'm not married."

The laird turned toward Drostan, and I swallowed as I watched the way he grinned at his son.

"Ye are no married, ye say? Ye must come from a fine family if yer cousin has married a MacChristy son. My Drostan is in need of a wife."

I swallowed so the ale I had in my mouth wouldn't come up my nose. Before I could panic and respond even more inappropriately, Callum reached over and grasped onto my hand, stepping in to take care of the situation for me.

"No, she is no married, but she is betrothed."

Laird Macaslan's face changed once more, his stern lines setting in, his smile evaporating in a second. It reminded me of one of those terrifying mimes that can change their expression as they wave their hand up and down over their face. It was truly unsettling.

"Betrothed? To who?"

Callum didn't release my hand. Instead, he raised it to his lips and kissed my fingers gently, winking at me in a clear plea for me to keep my mouth shut.

"To me."

Chapter 32

Orick's return to Fionn and Shona's was a somber one, but this time instead of an unwelcome glare, Shona greeted him with ale and a tender hug. He suspected Fionn had warned her to be kind.

"Did ye find the lass? Were ye able to help her?"

He followed Shona inside and gratefully accepted the ale and food she offered him. He didn't know if he'd ever been so weary in his life.

"Aye, I found her. While I was no able to save her, I did offer her comfort in the last moments of her life."

Shona sat down beside him and patted his hand gently.

"'Tis all any of us can ask for in this life—someone to sit with us as we leave this earth. Who was she to ye? How did ye know her?"

Fionn stepped from the corner of the room to join them while he chided his wife.

"Shona, canna ye see how tired the man is? He knew the lass. He may no want to speak of her so soon."

"'Tis alright." Orick lifted his head and managed a small smile. His heart did hurt for Maidie or Marion as he knew her in the end, but more than that, he was grateful they found one another before it was too late.

"She was my sister, though the last I saw her, I was twelve and she no more than sixteen."

It was true enough. The true story he didn't have the strength to tell. Fionn and Shona weren't owed it anyway.

"Ach, man. I'm verra sorry for yer loss. How did ye know 'twas her when I spoke of the lass?" Fionn reached for his cup and refilled it.

Orick shrugged. His fatigue seemed to make the small lie easier to tell.

"'Twas a feeling."

"Aye? Well, take heart in knowing ye were there for her at the end."

Orick smiled and nodded as he stood from the table.

"Aye, I do."

Shona stood and walked with him to the doorway of his room.

"Ye are welcome to stay as long as ye like. Mayhap, ye need some time to mend from yer loss before ye carry on?"

He didn't need time. Idleness didn't heal loss, and it wasn't what Maidie would have wanted from him.

"No, though I thank ye. I'll leave come morning.

Once he finished eating, Laird Macaslan left quickly, making it very apparent to everyone that he was in no hurry to release Lennox and Griffith. It didn't take long for Callum and Adwen to follow after him, leaving Jane and me alone in the room with Drostan.

A few long awkward minutes followed. Then, just as Jane stood and I followed suit, Drostan spoke. He had orange-colored hair and yellowish skin that made him look ill. He was short, fat, and frankly, rather repulsive.

"'Tis a shame ye are already betrothed. I believe Da wanted ye as my bride."

I coughed uncomfortably and moved around the table next to Jane for comfort. My mouth had already gotten me in enough trouble. Luckily, Jane's tongue no longer seemed tied.

"Yes, such a shame, but you heard Callum, she's already taken. Goodnight, Drostan. Would you have someone show us to our rooms, please?"

Jane didn't give him a chance to answer or send us assistance before she had me by the arm and pulled me from the room.

Chapter 33

"That is exactly why I told you not to say anything." Jane's voice rose at least three octaves higher than normal as she slipped into the bedchamber assigned to me and screeched like a banshee.

I whirled on her, giving her every bit of frustration right back. I'd already reached my limit for the day as well.

"No way. Don't do that. This isn't my fault. What was I supposed to say to him? I wasn't the one who lied. That was Callum. Why would he say that?"

Jane exhaled, leaned against the door, and pinched her thumb and forefinger together against her nose. I stayed back and allowed her the time she needed to cool down.

Eventually, she spoke more calmly, her tone much less high and squeaky.

"You're right. It was Callum. He did it so that Laird Macaslan wouldn't mention the very thing Drostan just did in the dining hall. But it doesn't matter. As soon as Lennox and Griffith are released, we can be back on our way home, and this entire thing will be forgotten."

Something clanked loudly in the hall outside my bedroom, followed by a loud hushing sound from Adwen before Jane stepped out of the way to allow him and Callum to enter. I could tell by the tightness of Callum's jaw and the shade of his face things with the laird hadn't gone well.

"What?" I asked the question as Jane sat herself down on the floor and answered for them.

"He still hasn't released them."

Callum spoke between gritted teeth. "Damn the bastard. He doesna have the right to keep them, no now that their debt is paid. Though the truth is he has them, and there is precious little we can do to force his hand, no with just the two of us."

Jane leapt up to her feet and started pacing the room as if she were looking for a weapon. "Well, how long is he going to keep them? He can't keep them forever, can he?"

Adwen spoke from the shadows of the room, his voice calmer than the rest of us.

"No, he canna, but he can keep them for far longer than we can allow him to. He has made Callum a proposal. 'Twould result in their immediate release."

Jane nodded and held her hands up in question. "Okay, great. That's wonderful. What is it?"

Adwen stepped into the candlelight. His aggravated expression made me nervous.

"Ye tell her Callum. I doona have the heart for it. "

I laughed uncomfortably, hoping he meant to tease me unnecessarily.

"Don't have the heart for what? Come on guys, one of you just spit it out."

Callum stepped away from the door and neared me, reaching a hand out to touch the side of my arm.

"He wishes for us to get married here, lass. Tomorrow."

"Ha." I did laugh then, a full, hearty laugh that Jane had to shush with her hand before I had the opportunity to wake up the whole castle.

Once I regained control of myself, I spoke again.

"No way. Just tell him *no*. Tell him that we wish to get married at Cagair. Extend a damn invitation if you want to. And then, demand that he let your father and brother go. After we are gone awhile, send him a letter and tell him we broke up."

Callum squeezed my arm as if he expected that to soothe me. I jerked away from his grip.

"'Tis no so simple, Gillian. Ye doona understand Laird Macaslan. He is no a man to be toyed with. He doesna make idle threats. If I wish to have my da and brother released by year's end, 'tis the only choice I have."

"It's the only choice you have?" I repeated myself for good measure as my panic rose. "Isn't this my choice, as well? Why did you even tell him that in the first place? I met you less than twelve hours ago."

I heard a growl from the corner of the room and looked over to see that Adwen looked just as displeased about the idea as me.

"Ye canna do this, brother. For Orick's sake if naught else."

Callum stepped away from me and turned to face Adwen while Jane came and stood next to me in comfort. She waited until I looked at her then scrunched her nose and shook her head as if to say, '*don't worry*'.

"Will the both of ye no wait and allow me to finish? I've no intention of marrying the lass, no really. Part of the agreement was that he would release Da and Griffith so they can attend the ceremony. Once they are free, we will all make our escape before the ceremony. I've no wish to steal Orick's lass. I just dinna wish to see the lass forced into a marriage with Drostan."

I wanted to weep with relief.

"So no wedding. Orick's not going to show back up here and find me married to you?"

"No, lass. I swear to ye. Though ye shall have to go along with the ruse until just before, aye?"

I nodded. I'd spent my fair share of time pretending it was my wedding day as a young girl. I could do the same tomorrow with no problem.

"Sure, you got it. I will play along and be the happiest bride in the world tomorrow. As long as I don't end up standing at the end of the aisle across from you."

Callum laughed and made his way to the door.

"I will try to no take offense to that, lass. Doona worry, ye willna end up married to me. No unless he holds a knife to each of our throats and forces the ceremony to go forward. And even Laird Macaslan is no as cruel as that."

Chapter 34

Macaslan territory didn't lie far from Shona and Fionn's. Orick left before sunrise and reached the edge of Macaslan's land by midday. He couldn't wait to see everyone, but it worried him to see Adwen riding toward him alone even before he reached the castle.

Orick called out to him as they met. "What's the matter with ye?"

"I told Callum 'twas a fool's plan. Laird Macaslan has seen to make trouble with us long before this day. They're all in the chapel, and he has Da and Griffith still in chains no to be taken off until Gillian and Callum's wedding vows are said."

"Gillian and Callum? What the hell did ye allow to happen over the course of a day?"

Orick took off at a gallop toward the chapel as Adwen hurried to keep up.

"Orick, ye need to slow down so we can talk of a plan of action. 'Twas no Gillian's doing. I swear the lass is but a moment away from reaching for the nearest sword and running Callum straight through. He told her it wouldna come to this, but there she is now, standing at the end of the aisle with him just exactly where he swore to her she wouldna be."

Orick reluctantly slowed his horse and spoke to Adwen in a voice so disgruntled he could hardly recognize it as his own.

"Ye need to tell me what has happened here. I still doona know how any of this has come about."

Adwen reached across the expanse between their horses and whacked him so hard across the back he struggled to stay on his horse.

"Canna ye see that I doona have time to tell ye anything unless ye wish to allow Gillian to marry my brother?"

"No." The very thought made Orick's skin hot with rage. "I doona wish for her to marry Callum."

"Aye, I know it. 'Tis why I snuck away to meet with ye. There is no one inside the chapel save Laird Macaslan, Drostan, Callum, Gillian, Jane, and a few guards with Da and Griffith. I doona think 'twill be difficult to take the guards. Laird Macaslan and Drostan willna raise a sword, for they know they willna win a fight. Laird Macaslan has others fight his battles and always has. We can stop the wedding and get Da and Griffith back with no bloodshed, so doona hurt a soul."

Orick pulled on his horse's reins outside the chapel, dismounted quickly and walked toward the chapel with his hand near his sword.

"I will no hurt the guards nor Laird Macaslan and his son. If Callum falls on my fist, I canna be blamed for it."

Adwen laughed as they neared the doorway together.

"I'd say he deserves it. Are ye ready?"

They pushed the main doors of the church open together.

I understood that Callum had no choice now that Laird Macaslan had lost his mind and was set on forcing this absurd marriage on us, but it didn't make me any less angry with him. I didn't know if there'd ever been a bride with such a pissed off look on her face in the entire history of the world.

I wondered what would happen if I simply said *no*? I thought about it and then I looked over at Drostan, staring at us with a chunky smile that made my skin crawl. I imagined he would be ready and willing to take Callum's place. Then it wouldn't matter what my answer was.

My only source of comfort was the portal back at Cagair Castle. I'd not missed the fact that Adwen was strangely absent from the chapel or that Jane seemed uncharacteristically calm about the wedding. I would hold out hope that Adwen would save the day up until the very last minute. But if he didn't end this in time, then I would be high-tailing it to Orick where I would beg him to disappear into the future with me.

We could see where our relationship went there, but I wouldn't stay in the seventeenth century a minute longer than I had to if I wound up married to Callum.

I could hear the ceremony start, but it sounded like little more than the hum of a bee as I kept my attention glued to the doorway, hoping with every breath that the doors would open and this bizarre nightmare would end.

When the doors did finally swing toward us, I squealed so loudly that everyone in the chapel turned to look at me rather than Adwen and Orick.

It worked to their advantage, providing the time they needed to walk up behind the men who stood watching Lennox and Griffith and successfully knock both of them out with the hilt of their swords.

Unfortunately, what they didn't see was the group of Laird Macaslan's men who quickly filed into the chapel behind them. Within moments, they had both Adwen and Orick in their grasp with a knife to their throats.

Jane screamed at the sight. Her screech was enough to entice Laird Macaslan into action for the first time since Adwen and Orick's entry.

"Hush yer wails, woman. I doona intend to shed blood here. I swear it to ye. I dinna believe Callum for a moment, but we've readied this place for a wedding and one shall take place here this day. If no to Callum, then the lass shall marry Drostan, and she will stay here on Macaslan land."

I would rather eat my own limbs than marry Drostan Macaslan. "No. I'm not marrying, Drostan. I'm not marrying Callum, either. Isn't it up to my father to give permission that I marry or at the very least, the laird in the territory in which I reside?"

For a moment, Laird Macaslan looked concerned. Then he simply laughed and crossed his arms in amusement. I wanted to strangle him.

"I doona think ye are in a position to deny me, lass. I doona believe yer father lives. If he did, ye wouldna be traveling without him when ye are no married. And ye are marrying the laird of yer territory, so I am no in the wrong. Still, I am no an unkind man. Ye are free to marry any unmarried man in this room. I only see the two."

"There's three." Orick spoke up despite the blade against his throat.

Laird Macaslan laughed again and waved a dismissive hand at the man who held Orick. The man released Orick instantly.

"Orick, I know that ye've always thought yerself a MacChristy, but ye are no one. Ye doona have any land of yer own and willna ever have any. Ye are little more than a pauper. Still, I told the lass she could have her choice."

Laird Macaslan turned to me as my heart sped up so fast I thought I might faint.

"Laird MacChristy, Drostan, or the pauper? With two, ye will live a life of fortune—with the last one, a life of certain ruin. The choice is yers."

I didn't hesitate.

"The pauper, please. Any day of the week."

Chapter 35

A week ago, I thought the man riding next to me was dead. I didn't know any sort of time traveling portal existed, and I certainly saw my life heading in a very different direction. I didn't feel like a bride. Today wouldn't go down as the happiest day of my life.

Instead, it seemed that by marrying Orick, we'd taken a huge step backward. As if we could both feel the oddity in it, the unnatural progression of our relationship and the lack of enthusiasm on both our parts created a strain between us. It was more than that though. Orick's mind lay elsewhere. I suspected it had to do with Marion, but I knew he would talk about it when he was ready.

After the ceremony, both of us wanted to get as far away from Laird Macaslan as possible, so we split from the rest of the group and headed back toward McMillan territory. Adwen, Jane, and Callum first planned to escort Lennox and Griffith safely out of the region, so it would be weeks before we met with them back at Cagair Castle.

The time away from the rest of them would allow us the time to decide where things went from here. In all honesty, the sudden pressure of being married made me want to run back through the portal and pretend that the last few days had never happened. But I knew that wasn't an option. Orick would follow me right through. He deserved better anyway.

We made the return journey to McMillan territory in half the time it took us on the outbound trip, only stopping for one night and only then for a few hours. When we did stop, we were both so tired we hardly said two words to each other. While we did sleep close to each other, there wasn't so much as a kiss shared between us.

I wondered how things would be when we rode up to Gregor and Isobel's; how Orick would behave toward me since no one knew of our recent nuptials. It would say a lot about him, whatever he did, and I only hoped he wouldn't turn into someone totally different than he'd been on the road.

We must have been thinking along the same lines for he turned toward me just as we neared the village.

"Can we stop for a moment, Gillian? I wish to talk to ye."

I nodded. As we pulled our horses to a stop and dismounted, he came over and gently reached for one of my hands. It was the first real sign of affection I'd seen from him since we left. He led me over to the base of a tree and bent to sit down in front of it. I joined him.

"Part of me feels I should apologize, to beg ye to forgive me for no keeping ye from what happened. I invited ye back here, I should've protected ye. 'Tis what I wished to do first, but the more I thought on it, the more I realized 'twas no my fault. I couldna have known what would happen. And I dinna think ye would appreciate the apology."

"You're right. I wouldn't appreciate it. It's not your fault at all." Truthfully, had he sat me down and apologized, in all likelihood, it would have infuriated me. The fact that he'd worked that out on his own meant he knew me better than I expected.

"Aye, then I'm glad I dinna apologize, for I canna really be sorry for it. 'Twas no more my choice than yers. I couldna make sense of how I felt before but, as we near the village, I ken that more than anything, I feel gratitude."

"Gratitude?"

"Aye, thank ye for choosing me. Ye could have married Callum, and he would have released ye. He would no have made ye consummate the marriage, and he would have let ye return to yer home. But had ye chosen Callum, I couldna be with ye."

He took a deep, nervous breath, and I squeezed his hand in comfort.

"I offer ye just what Callum would have. Ye doona have to stay with me nor consummate the marriage until ye are ready. Ye may leave whenever ye wish, but I hope that yer choice at least means we are no ready to end what we started only a few days ago."

"No." I shook my head and leaned in to kiss him. "I don't want it to end. I'm just not sure how to proceed. I can't pretend that I'm ready to be married to you. We're not there yet."

"Aye, I know. Let's no tell Isobel, Gregor, or Cooper yet. I think it fine if we give ourselves some time, aye? We will greet them and then spend the day resting on our own. Tomorrow, if ye like, we can head toward Cagair Castle, and there we can spend time alone together."

With one conversation, the tension between us vanished and things felt as comfortable as they had been days before. He understood things about me that I'd never expressed to him, and I appreciated his thoughtfulness more than he knew.

Everything was happening more quickly than I was comfortable with, but I could already tell that I was far luckier in my choice of a husband than most.

Chapter 36

Orick stood in the sitting room of the inn quietly out of sight while Isobel spoke to Cooper. He knew if the lad saw him, he would use him as an excuse to stay.

"Do I have to go back home already? Please let me stay a little bit longer. I could stay the night if you would let me."

Isobel stayed firm with the child, and Orick was grateful for it. He was far too tired to handle the lad's endless energy this night.

"No, ye must go back. They need their rest. Get on with ye. We will see ye tomorrow."

He listened until the child reluctantly hugged Isobel and then mounted his small horse and rode away. When Isobel walked by, he reached for her.

"Ach, are ye trying to scare me to death? I thought ye were up in yer room having a rest."

Orick nodded and kept a hand around Isobel's arm so he could lead her up the stairs. "Aye, I was trying to."

"What kept ye from it? I sent Cooper away so ye wouldna be disturbed."

Reaching the top of the stairs, Orick stopped them just outside Gillian's door. "Do ye no hear that noise, Isobel?"

The sound of Gillian snoring travelled easily through the doorway.

Isobel shrugged at him and stepped away.

"I doona ken what ye wish for me to do about the lassie's breathing. Though I can see why it kept ye awake."

Orick shook his head and crossed his arms as he blocked Isobel's path. "The snoring doesna bother me. What kept me awake was hearing that noise travels so plainly through the wee walls. Ye knew that when ye told me to visit Gillian's room. Does that mean that ye heard everything that night?"

Isobel smiled at him unabashedly.

"Gregor was dead asleep. He dinna hear a thing. I heard only wee bits and pieces so doona worry. 'Tis no as if the two of ye carried on for verra long anyway. Though I doona think ye should visit her tonight. She sounds like she needs her rest."

Isobel squeezed by him and laughed quietly to herself the rest of the way down the hall.

The soft touch of lips against his brow seemed the most pleasant way to wake if he ever knew one. His eyes fluttered open to see Gillian standing above him as her pup crawled onto his chest and started licking at his neck.

"Good morning."

He lifted his head and looked toward the window in disbelief. It seemed as if he'd only just fallen asleep. "It canna be morning yet."

Gillian nodded. Only then did he notice that she was already dressed, her hair pulled up and her riding boots on.

"Yes, just barely though. Is it okay if we get going soon? I'm anxious to get back to Cagair."

He could sleep until late in the day if left undisturbed, but he didn't mind being awakened by Gillian. He was just as eager to get to Cagair Castle as she was, to escape from everyone but her and try his hardest to win her heart.

For he knew with certainty, even in the short time that that they'd known one another, that she had his completely.

Chapter 37

"Marion, the lass I went after, she was my sister."

"What?" I lay with my head against his chest, snuggled into him as we camped for the last night before reaching Cagair Castle. Each day Orick made a point of sharing some part of himself with me—stories of his childhood, the tragedy that befell his family and how he met Adwen, funny stories about years of travelling with the MacChristy's—each story helped him unfold before me, but none of them surprised me as much as this. "I thought Marion was the woman who saved you after you fell?"

He shifted just slightly so that he could look down at me. The emotion in his eyes was visible.

"Aye. She was. Her real name is Maidie. She dinna tell me it until just before she died in my arms."

I pulled away and twisted so that I could lean on my arm and look directly at him. "How? I thought she died with your parents."

"I thought that she did. When I arrived back at our home, my parents were lying dead in the entryway. I dinna venture inside further—I couldna bear to see more than I already had. I assumed Maidie was dead. I lit the place afire and ran. It explains so much of how Marion was, though I never thought it possible for a moment."

I nodded, understanding as I remembered his talk of how secluded Marion was, how she distrusted everyone and had lived alone for so many years.

"She saw what you did and ran, only she didn't have an Adwen to save her."

"No. I was far luckier than she. Though 'tis a blessing we found each other in the end."

I reached up to brush away a tear that pooled in the corner of his eye. He grabbed my wrist as I did so, slowly bringing my palm to his mouth so he could kiss it.

"Did she know all along who you were?"

"No. She dinna have any more reason to think it possible than I. When I found her dying in the woods, I told her that I'd remembered and that my name was no Craig but Orick, and she knew then. She meant to travel to our home, and 'tis there where I buried her."

"I'm so sorry, Orick." I leaned in and kissed his brow.

"Ye doona need to be sorry. I am sad for it and will be for some time, but I'm grateful she found me and that I was there for her when she died and was able to bring her home."

The events of Orick's life made my own heartaches seem quite trivial. He'd been through so much, so many different times, and still he lived with his heart open. He didn't shut people out just because he was afraid of being hurt. I was a coward, and I was tired of it.

After all of the things he'd shared with me, I could try to gather the courage to do the same with him.

"Why have you told me all of this? None of it can be very easy for you to talk about."

I could see by his expression he thought it an odd question.

"No, but most things are no meant to come easy. I've found the conversations that do are also often verra meaningless."

I realized it was very much the way I lived my life, keeping only things that meant nothing close, so that I had nothing to lose.

"You're so brave, Orick. Being around you makes me feel like such a coward."

He reached down and tilted my chin up so I would look at him before he ducked and kissed me.

"A coward, lass? No ever have I seen signs of cowardice in ye."

"It's not in the things I do but in the way I allow myself to feel. My heart is a coward."

"'Tis only that yer heart is slower to open. Just like the buds of the most beautiful flowers. Ye just need time."

I moved into him so close that I could hear the beat of his heart in my ear. "Doesn't it bother you that I haven't shared anything with you—that you open up and I don't return the trust?"

"Ye will when yer ready."

I kissed him, slow and long and with enough fervor that we both came away from it breathless. "I will. I promise one day I will crack open like a clamshell, and you'll learn more about me than you ever wanted to. But not tonight."

Chapter 38

I was too shocked the last time I visited Cagair Castle during this century to take notice of the lack of people around it but, after being at Macaslan Castle and seeing the number of men and women who worked for him, it seemed odd. In fact, the closer we got, I realized it was seemingly vacant.

"Is there anyone here? Where are the workers or guards or maids that help Callum run this place?"

Orick shook his head as he dismounted then turned to help me off of Grock. I reached to pat the horse's neck before I slid off him, bending to thank him for the ride. I'd grown rather fond of the beast and, to my complete surprise, my rear end, while still sore, seemed to be much more accustomed to riding than it had been.

"When Callum is away, he sends the rest away as well. He thinks if he gets to enjoy his travels so should the villagers that work so hard for him. He's a fair man, if no a damned fool for thinking he could marry ye."

I laughed and walked with him as we led our horses to the stables.

"Does he just leave it unlocked?"

"Aye. 'Tis so isolated that none will disturb it. And old man Tom comes up from the village each day to ensure all is well."

I could almost see the relief in Grock's eyes as he spotted his stall in the stables. He would be happy for the rest after such a long journey.

"Will Tom assume everything is not well when he sees us inside the castle?"

"No." Orick took my hand as we walked out of the stables. "I'll speak to him before it can cause him worry. Ye have a choice to make, lass. I dinna grow up in a castle, no before I fell in with the MacChristy's nor after. To sleep in a castle makes my skin itch in a way I doona care for. Adwen suffers from the same affliction, though Callum's adjusted to the castle well enough. When Adwen was laird here, I stayed in the stable house. 'Tis there that I feel the most at home.

"If ye wish to stay separately, I understand. I ken that we dinna have a choice on the way here, but I willna assume just because we are married that ye wish to share my bed. I can prepare a room for ye in the castle. Even if ye wish to stay together, 'tis up to ye where we sleep. If ye prefer the castle, 'tis there where we shall stay."

Nights of sleeping in each other's arms on the way here, nights of holding and kissing but not truly touching had me itching for sex in a way unfamiliar to me. I knew it must have done the same to him—he was just too polite to say so outright.

I reached for him, pulling his face into my hands as I kissed him and then wrapped my arms around him to speak into his ear.

"I do want to share your bed, Orick. I have wanted to since the first night you showed up at the back door in the rain." I laughed, thinking back on my dreams of him. "Truthfully, I wanted to long before that. And the stable house is absolutely fine. I married the pauper, remember, not the laird."

His breath caught, and he pulled me closer as his hands wound into my hair. He pulled my head back so he could kiss me once more. His lips moved skillfully over mine until my legs were shaky and my breathing came fast. When he pulled away, I could see the need in his eyes.

"Just so I doona misunderstand ye, ye doona mean sleep as we have done so before, aye? Ye mean…"

I nodded and reached down to tease him, gently running my fingers up his thigh.

"Yes, Orick. I think it's high time we consummate this marriage of ours."

Chapter 39

"Truly?"

He asked the question like he simply couldn't believe it. His excitement was adorable.

"Yes, truly." I laughed and kissed him once more. "It would no longer shame me since we are married. Orick, I want to be with you."

He groaned and held my face tightly in his hands, looking at me with an enthusiasm I'd never seen from him before.

"And I ye, lass. Can ye wait a short while? I havena been inside the stable house in a long time. I doona wish to bed ye amongst the cobwebs and filth. Allow me to clean it and prepare a bath for us."

"The both of us?" Orick was astonishingly tall and his home rather small. "It would have to take up half the room to hold the both of us."

He winked and pulled away from me, eager to get started. "Aye, it nearly does. I shall hurry as fast as I can, Gillian."

"Okay. I'll just wait over on the castle steps."

He smiled and watched me as I walked over to the steps.

I had a penchant for being able to sleep anywhere. I was slumped over and out within five minutes.

When I woke, it was to the touch of Orick's arms slipping underneath me so that he could lift me from my napping roost on the stone steps.

"Oh wow, my sleeping and snoring is just exactly what you needed to get your engine revving, I bet."

He pursed his lips together in confusion. "I doona ken what ye mean. Yer snoring doesna bother me, truly. Ye'll be wide awake soon enough. Come inside with me."

He carried me through the doorway and then set me on my feet. Everything inside was spotless and perfect. A fire burned in the corner. A comically large tub sat near it, filled three-quarters of the way with water so steaming I couldn't imagine how he'd heated it all. The bed was turned back and comfortable looking, and on a small table, he'd laid out cheese and ale for snacking. My pulse quickened at the mere sight of everything, and my heart warmed at the thought he'd put into it.

"How long did I sleep?"

He shrugged and smiled at my reaction.

"I doona know. I was glad ye slept, though, for I felt badly for taking so long."

"Don't. It's wonderful." I smiled as I felt him step toward me, his front touching my back as his arms came around my waist, and he bent so that his chin rested on my shoulder.

"As are ye." He nibbled at my collarbone before dragging his sweet kisses up my neck as his breathing escalated and his hands started to roam over my front.

I gasped as his hands gripped at my breast, and I reached behind me to start working on my own laces. Seeing what I was doing, he pushed my hands away so that he could undo them for me. His hands moved quickly down the laces, but once the dress was loose, he paused.

"Turn toward me, Gillian. I want to see ye."

I did, pulling at the fabric near my waist so that it would drop. I still had my hair pulled up from the ride but, as the dress dropped, Orick reached behind me and pulled my hair loose, running his fingers through it so that it draped around my shoulders.

"Yer hair, lass. 'Tis a thing of beauty, just like every bit of ye."

I stood naked before him. Quickly I grew cold from standing in the open, and he pointed to the tub as he started to disrobe himself.

"Get in and I'll join ye."

I enjoyed this side of him. While he was always confident, I liked to see him state so plainly what he wanted. In this moment, he wasn't thinking about everyone else. I found it insanely attractive.

The water felt amazing as I slipped inside. It was so deep I had to sit on my knees to keep from going under. If I wanted to relax and lay back in the water, I would have to do so on Orick's lap. Although, I suspected that's why he filled it as full as he did.

"I'm afraid once you get in here the water's going to splash over the side, and you'll have to hold me up so I don't drown."

I watched as he removed his shoes first, then his shirt and finally his pants. I'd always thought the expression '*the size of the shoes shows the size of the man*' was probably a bunch of hogwash—not in Orick's case. I swallowed and looked down at my thighs in the water to keep from showing my nerves.

He didn't seem to notice and, once he was naked, stepped into the tub behind me, sliding to his bottom and reaching for me to pull me securely onto his lap. I lay back against him as he kissed my neck.

"Doona worry about drowning, lass. I'll hold ye right here."

He reached over the side for a rag and wet it before running it up and down my front, the roughness of the rag scratching my skin deliciously. The touch of it seemed to tease me until finally I could take no more. I wanted his hands on me, in me—I wanted him to send me spiraling.

"Touch me, Orick. Just drop the rag and touch me."

I felt what my words did to him, and the rod in my back only heightened my need for him. He obliged me quickly using one arm to hold me against him as his other hand dipped beneath the water, reaching in between my legs to massage me there. I panted and writhed against him, climbing as he quickened the pace of his fingers.

When I peaked, he groaned into my ear, standing from the tub as he grabbed a blanket to wrap us in. He pulled me up with him, turning me so that I would wrap my legs around him as he carried me to the bed.

He said nothing. He didn't need to, our bodies responded to each other in a way words never could.

We fell roughly onto the bed. The weight of him sent my breath out in a sudden rush before he lifted himself for entry. My legs opened on instinct. With our bodies still wet and my center still ready, he plunged into me with so much force that I cried out from the size of him.

"I'm sorry." His words were choked, painful. "I canna pull out from ye, lass."

He'd mistaken my scream for pain. While it had hurt, I didn't want him to stop for a moment. It hurt so good.

"I don't want you to."

That was the only permission he needed, and he took me like a man who'd gone a very long time without such intimacy. I reveled in his need for me, in the desperate urgency of his every move. He carried me upward with his passion, and together we crumbled and shook against one another.

Chapter 40

Gillian thought he was sleeping. Orick could tell by the way she didn't move a muscle while she whispered to him beneath her breath. Her feet stayed wrapped around his legs, her arm draped across his chest. The only thing that moved besides Gillian's lips was the wee pup that lay curled between his legs, but he didn't dare move himself for fear she'd stop talking.

She reminded him of an octopus, the strange sea dwelling creature he saw caught on one of he and Adwen's seafaring ventures, long ago. She was wrapped so tightly around him. He hoped she wouldn't ever let go.

If the secret words she whispered to him now were any indication, she didn't mind being his wife overmuch.

"You want to know how I feel about you? It's so much easier to tell you when you can't hear me. But maybe you can, maybe in some way your subconscious will understand what I say, and you'll feel it when you wake. That seems so much better than telling you to your face.

"I wasn't always so cold. I used to be quite the artsy romantic. I could fall hard and fast, and I did more than once as a teenager. No one like you—they were boys not men. I have a feeling you were never really a boy."

Oh, the lass had no idea. Just because he'd been faster at it than Adwen, it didn't mean he wasn't slow to mature. He'd been a boy for far longer than he'd been a man.

"I loved everyone, everything, and I was headed in a million different directions. I wanted to paint, I wanted to act, I wanted to be the world's greatest chef. I just never imagined that things wouldn't work out the way I wanted them to.

"And then, my Dad got sick and he died. Six months later my Mom followed him. Losing him was enough. Then I watched as my picture-of-health mother, in her mid-fifties, died of heartbreak. She should have lived for thirty more years. It angered me, it terrified me, and more than anything, it made me determined to never, ever let that happen to me.

"After that I just stopped—all of the dreaming, all of the falling fast—I just stopped everything. I stopped feeling or living past the most shallow of relationships or experiences. Anything that I really needed to feel, I put in a painting. Until now."

He wanted to turn to her, and speak to her, but he knew she'd stop, and he wanted her to say all she needed to. He kept his eyes closed and listened.

"Before they died, I imagined you, I wanted you every single day. Maybe not you, per se. Even my imagination couldn't dream up someone as handsome, but I imagined the person you are—the kind, loyal to a fault, understatedly funny, ridiculously awesome in bed, hung like a racehorse man that you are—I dreamed of you. I dreamed of marrying.

"After their deaths, I let the dream go. I stopped imagining anything past the end of the week. Now, I'm imagining things thirty years from now, every one of them spent with you.

"You want to know how I feel about you? I'm crazy about you. I love you. I know I do, but it's so hard for me to admit. It's been so long since I've allowed myself to feel it, and you're my worst fear brought to life. You could destroy me. I don't want to become my mother.

He wished she had the strength to tell him all of these things at a time when he could respond—when he could turn to her and comfort her fears. But to do so now would damage the trust she'd placed in him, so he would have to go forward pretending he didn't know, pretending that he'd heard nothing.

He hoped at least, she'd eased her own mind. With time, Gillian would share more with him. He knew that with certainty now. There would be a time when she would share everything she'd just told him now. He would be right there to reciprocate and listen when she was ready.

As if the pup knew the moment Gillian's speech was finished, Toby latched down on Orick's big toe causing him to jerk up in the bed at the shock of it. He admired the way Gillian lay on her back and stretched sleepily, still managing to look up at him with tired eyes.

"Good morning. How did you sleep?"

He leaned down to kiss her. "I've no slept better in my life, but I am not ready to rise from this bed just yet."

Chapter 41

The next day, we made love two more times before noon. When we did finally rise, we didn't wander far, just out onto the lawn where we played with Toby for a long while. Orick loved the little mess and would wrestle with the pup until Toby would just give out from exhaustion.

It was during one of his short little rests, where he plopped down on the grass and went to sleep, that Orick came over and pulled me down on the grass so that we each lay on one side of Toby.

"I've been thinking, lass."

"Have you?" I smiled playfully at him as if that surprised me. I doubted that he ever stopped thinking.

"Aye, always. If ye stay with me, Gillian, we must settle some matters between us. When and where will we live? What will each of us do? I ken ye time traveling women well enough to know that ye are no content to stay idle. Ye must each have yer own purpose, and I understand. I wondered if ye'd tell me, what ye saw for us?"

I'd not placed much thought in it. I knew myself well enough to know that if I did, I'd freak myself out thinking in the long term. I knew he was right though. It didn't matter if it freaked me out, there were many things we would have to decide, and all of that would be so much easier for the both of us if I would quit being such a pansy and be honest with him. I would have to face my own fears in order to relieve his. I could tell each time he said, '*if ye stay,*' he still very much wondered if I would.

"Orick, I'm going to stay. I married you. While it wasn't the ceremony I envisioned—outdoors with flowers and the sea roaring in the background—it was the ceremony that I got. And forced into it or not, I take that seriously. Besides, I'm kind of crazy about you."

He smiled and reached to pull me near him, but I held out a hand to stop him, not wanting to squish Toby.

"Ye are crazy about me? 'Tis a good thing?"

"Yes, it's one of the best things. I know you need more, but that's all you'll get out of me today on the feelings front."

He shook his head and said words that took my breath away. I already knew how he felt. He showed it all the time.

"I love ye, Gillian. I doona care if it takes ye a fortnight or a year to tell me the same, it willna change my feelings. Ye are allowed to need time. I'm glad ye are no leaving, but ye still have no answered my question."

"Right." I'd gotten sidetracked. "Would you believe me if I said I hadn't thought that far ahead?"

His eyes grew wide as he nodded as if it were no surprise to him at all. "Aye, I believe I would. It doesna matter, for I have thought much on it. May I make ye a proposal?"

I shifted to sit cross-legged so I could look at him. I wanted to pay close attention.

"Yes."

"There was a time when I dinna think I would ever leave Adwen's side. Now I ken that I canna ever go back to it. If he needs me I'll come, but I must live my own life—a life spent with ye. I ken that we've still much to learn about one another, but I doona think ye are a lass suited to this life, no all the time."

I didn't either, but I planned to make the best out of it, to try as hard as I could for him. "I'll try. I really will."

Orick shook his head and reached to squeeze my hand.

"Ye shouldna have to. I doona think I've told ye, but I spent a few night's in New York City with Adwen, Jane, and Cooper."

"What?" For the life of me, I couldn't picture Adwen and Orick in that concrete jungle.

"Aye, and do ye wish to know something else? I loved it. So many of the things from yer own time, things I should have found strange, I took great pleasure in. I think 'twould be easier for me to live there than ye here, though I hope that we could mayhap live our lives in a little of both."

While I truly hadn't placed much thought in it, I had never seen Orick living in my own time as an option. The thought delighted me to no end. "Do you mean it? You would do that? Live away from Adwen, Jane, Cooper, Isobel...everybody?"

"Aye. 'Tis a bonny thing about Cagair. We can live in both times and travel back and forth as we need to. 'Twould work well for the others, too."

"It would, but what would you do there? I don't think you're one to sit idle either."

I could see Orick's enthusiasm at my question, and he quickly pushed himself up to sit opposite me.

"I've thought on this as well. My life has been spent in the service of others. While I am Adwen's friend, I grew up as the MacChristy's," he hesitated, "I doona ken the right word for it."

"I know what you mean. You were their man. You did whatever they needed."

"Aye. I believe I would still like to be there for others. I've an idea for Cagair."

I couldn't wait to hear what he said. I wondered if he found me as surprising as I found him. "What is it?"

"The castle has far too many rooms for my liking. Even if we had a few bairns, many would still lay empty. 'Tis as beautiful a place as I've ever seen. Why doona we open our own inn?"

The moment he said it, I couldn't believe I'd not thought of it myself. It was the perfect idea. I knew Orick birthed the idea out of care for me. He may have enjoyed his time in New York, but he was a simple man, a man who would miss many things about his life here. It would be a sacrifice for him to stay in the twenty-first century, even if we traveled back here often.

If he could do it for me, I could make a sacrifice for him as well.

"I would love that, but only if we don't live in the castle. Let's go forward and tell Aiden and Anne our plan, offer them residence in the castle? They can work for us, and they can be the ones to live in the castle. We will live in the stable house."

He crossed his arms as if he didn't believe me. "Gillian, I know what I said about castles, but I doona expect ye to live out here. Ye love the castle."

"Yes, but I also love this little place. It suits you much more, I think. It's the only way I'll agree to the inn."

He grinned and pulled me in close, pinching my bottom as he placed me on his lap.

"Aye, ye drive a hard bargain, lass, but naught could sound better to me."

Chapter 42

Cagair Castle—Present Day

"Where are you going?" I reached to pull on Orick's arm as he exited the stairwell and headed for the front of the castle. "We can just go in the back."

He nodded. "Aye, we could, but I doona think Aiden or Anne are expecting us. I doona care to scare them."

I actually thought it might be sort of fun to scare them, but I decided to follow his lead. I laced my fingers with his and walked up the castle's main steps beside him. Aiden must have seen us arrive for the door swung open as soon as we reached the top of the landing.

"Gillian and..." he reached for Orick's hand. "I'm sorry lad, I canna remember yer name."

I stepped in between them and wrapped my arms around Aiden's neck in greeting. "His name is Orick."

"Aye. Orick. I dinna expect to see either of ye for a week more, at least. Is everything okay? They were no lying, were they, Gillian?"

We followed him inside. I could tell Orick planned to let me lead the conversation.

"Yes, everything is fine. And no, much to my surprise, they weren't lying. Where's Anne?"

"Ah, Anne."

I didn't miss how his face reddened in sheepish embarrassment.

"She's only getting dressed. We took the day off, ye see."

"Oh, okay. Don't look so guilty." I laughed at him and pointed up the stairs. "Go and get her. I need to talk to you two about something."

While he ran upstairs to get Anne, Orick and I made our way into the sitting room. Orick sat down on the couch, but I wandered slowly about the room as we waited, peeking my head down the hallway, finding myself more impressed the more I looked.

"He's gotten a lot done in the last week. It doesn't look like there's much left."

"There's not. He's almost done." I turned toward Anne's voice as she ran toward me from the doorway, giving me a hug that nearly cracked my ribs. "I'm happy to see you, Gillian."

I laughed and pulled loose from her, moving quickly to seek shelter at Orick's side.

"I'm happy to see you too. I'm going to wait until Aiden gets seated to say anything though."

"Oh, that kind of talk, is it?" Anne pulled her face into one of seriousness and plopped down into a chair across from us.

Aiden quickly joined her. "Tell us about it, Gillian. We received yer letter, and the lawyer arrived the next day. Ye need to call him now that ye are back, but he dinna mind that ye were gone."

"Good." I made a mental note to remember to do that as I thought on how best to approach the subject. "So, have you booked any other jobs for after you're finished here?"

Aiden squeezed Anne's knee, and I knew it was to comfort her. She had to worry about it all the time.

"No, but 'twill be alright. It may be time that I do something else with my life."

"About that. What if the two of you stayed here and worked for me?"

Anne nearly came out of her chair. "What? Work for you how?"

"Orick and I are going to turn Cagair into an inn. We were wondering if Aiden would want to stay on in a sort of maintenance position, and you could work the front desk? The two of you could have the entire wing on the top floor of the right-hand side of the castle."

Anne squealed, but Aiden seemed to latch onto another part of my speech.

"Ye said, 'Orick and I.' Things must be going well between the two of ye then?"

He looked at the two of us and for the first time since entering, Orick spoke.

"Aye, she married me."

Aiden's eyes all but fell from his head, and Anne squealed so loudly that Toby took to growling at her feet in an effort to get her to shut up.

I knew we would have to return to the conversation about the inn later. The rest of the afternoon would be spent telling them everything that had happened.

Chapter 43

Three Weeks Later—A Road Near Conall Castle

"So what if we get there and the house isn't there?" I rode in the passenger seat next to Anne, Toby in my lap and a stack of invitations sitting in the back seat as we drove to where she swore Morna's house would be.

"Seriously, after everything you've seen in the last month, how can you possibly be so skeptical? She'll be here. I know she will. Trust me, ever since you sent that note forward about the lawyer, she's been much more accessible. She brought it to the castle herself. Said she was just dying to see inside."

As we continued down the long stretch of road, I finally spotted the house. "Yeah, I don't know. It's a problem. I shouldn't have doubted you. Do you think Aiden will manage to keep Orick out of the stable house?"

The day after we traveled forward, I commissioned Aiden to get to work on fixing up the stable house, making sure that it was modernized enough for me but that it also still had a few of the ancient flares that Orick would appreciate—an awkwardly large tub in the middle of the room being one of those.

"Yes, I think so. I don't think Orick has any real desire to see it before you're ready for him to. I think he enjoys the element of surprise."

I knew she was right. Any time I came close to accidentally dropping a hint about what was going inside, he would cover his ears and beg me to stop.

Aiden and his men made fantastic time on the castle itself, and renovations were complete within a week. Now, all that remained was the stable house where Orick and I would live, and Anne and I were off to Morna's to send a stack of invitations off into the past for the opening of the inn. We wanted everyone from then to be our first guests. It seemed appropriate given the love so many of them had for Cagair, and it would be an excellent way to let them know they were free to use the portal any time they wished.

As we neared the house, I could see the old woman standing in front and knew right away it was Morna. She had a friendly look to her, but I also found her to be rather ethereal-looking. I didn't doubt for a moment that she was the witch everyone said she was.

As soon as Anne saw her, she rolled down the window and stuck out her hand to wave dramatically.

Morna moved from her doorway and met us at the car as we pulled up.

"Anne, good to see ye, lass." She stuck her hand through the window and reached across Anne to get to my hand. "Ye must be, Gillian. What a pretty thing ye are. Ye remind me of myself once. I had red hair much as yers, though I know 'tis hard to tell now. Why doona the two of ye get out and come inside for a moment?"

Before I could tell her that we really needed to be getting back, Anne was out of the car and walking inside, making the decision for me.

Six hours later, we emerged from Morna's home, and I didn't care in the slightest that we would be driving back to Cagair all night in the dark. The conversation with Morna and her husband Jerry was beyond worth it.

"Ye two be careful driving back. I could give ye something to help ye stay awake if ye'd like. Ye are more than welcome to stay the night if ye'd rather."

"Oh no, it's okay. It was so nice to meet you. I really hope you'll come to Cagair with the rest of them."

She shook her head and waved a dismissive hand. "No, I'm afraid Jerry and I will be traveling then, but thank ye for the invitation."

Anne, who'd already said her goodbyes, carried the tray of baked goods she was sending with us back to the car and climbed in to wait for me.

"You're so welcome. Thank you for the stories and the food. And thanks for letting Toby come in. He sure did enjoy playing with Franklin."

I bent to pick up Toby and took a moment to scratch Morna's puppy on the top of his head. The two dogs looked almost identical, the only true exception being that while Toby's fur was fluffy and white, Franklin's was fluffy and tan.

"Oh, the wee fellows enjoyed it. Their play willna end just now. Will ye do me a favor, lass, and take Franklin with ye?

He's a gift for Cooper when he comes. His mother will no be pleased, but she will allow it. I've been watching. He sure grew attached to Toby. He needs a dog of his own."

I smiled and scooped up Franklin into my other arm.

"Are you sure?"

The old woman smiled and patted my back as she led me to the car.

"Aye, 'twas for Cooper that I got the pup, no myself. Have a safe journey back. Remember, I'm here if any of ye ever need me."

Chapter 44

One Week Later—Cagair Castle

Everyone arrived as we'd hoped. Cagair Castle was alive with a sense of joy and laughter and fellowship that it hadn't experienced in hundreds of years. Jane, along with Cooper's stepmother, Kathleen, kept crying at random intervals at every little thing. The sight of seeing the castle fully restored was just more than either of them could take without blubbering over.

Orick delighted in having everyone that he loved gathered together, but I could tell by nightfall of the day they arrived that being around so many people was already starting to weigh on him. It was the perfect time to show him all of Aiden's work. He'd finished it the day before and slipped me the key at breakfast this morning.

"Psst…" I stood in the shadows of the dining hall, trying my hardest to get Orick's attention without drawing everyone else's.

He didn't hear me.

I looked down at the floor and took notice of a small pebble. Picking it up, I chunked it as hard as I could in his direction. I meant to hit his shoulder but instead I hit his face. I saw him flinch before he turned to look in the direction from which the stone had come.

When he saw me waving him toward me, he gave me a crooked smile and stood.

He whispered when he saw my finger across my mouth.

"Are ye trying to put my eye out?"

I stood up and kissed the small red whelp on his cheek. "No, sorry about that. I was just trying to get your attention. Come with me."

I moved us quietly through the back hallways of the castle, exiting through the back door and running across the grass toward our new home with a firm grip on Orick's hand. When I got to the doorway, I stopped and faced him.

"It's ready. Do you want to see it?"

I could tell by the impatient twitch of his feet that he did.

"Aye, verra much. I doona think I would be able to sleep with so many around us in the castle."

I nodded and extended the key to him. "I know. But before you open it, I need to tell you something."

Only a month had passed since our wedding. I couldn't believe how my heart had changed in that time. I could no longer imagine hiding my love for him, and the thought of telling him didn't frighten me. Rather, it felt that if I didn't say the words, they would bubble out of me and I'd be forced to scream them.

"I love you. I'm sorry it's taken me so long to tell you, but I've loved you for much longer than today. As we start our life together here in this home, I don't want you to ever doubt that for a moment."

"Gillian."

He wrapped his arms around me and lifted me off the ground, pulling me into a kiss that left me ready to rip the key from his hand and open the door myself just so we could get inside and enjoy some privacy.

"I know ye love me, lass. I have no ever doubted it."

He unlocked the door and pushed his way inside, his arm still wrapped around me as he lowered me to my feet. The first thing he noticed was the tub.

"'Tis larger than the old one. I doona think ye should use it when I'm no around for ye are certain to drown in it."

I laughed and walked over to it. "It has a built-in seat, so I think I'll be okay. And the best part is, you don't have to heat the water up over a fire."

"Aye, 'tis wonderful."

Toby was inside the castle with Cooper so when Franklin ran up and jumped up on Orick's leg, he nearly jumped out of his skin. Then, he looked down to see the furry dog pawing at him to be picked up. He bent and obliged the creature right away.

"Did ye no think one was enough? Ye thought I needed one as well? A bairn or two and we will have to sleep on the floor for our bed will be filled."

Laughing, I scratched the pup behind the ears. "I wouldn't mind another dog but, no, this one isn't yours. Franklin belongs to Cooper. I was just keeping him here so he would remain a surprise until they were leaving. And so I would have time to tell his mother."

Orick nodded and released Franklin back onto the ground.

"I see."

I could tell by his short response that the rest of the room had finally grabbed his attention, and I stood back and allowed him time to explore. The wood and stone throughout looked much the same, only with the best modern things scattered throughout.

"Do you like it?"

"The only thing I like more is ye, lass. Must we go back right away, or can we spend some time here alone together. I've no ever had ye on a bed so big."

I laughed and moved to lock the front door, kicking off my shoes as I walked.

"We can stay here as long as you like. The party will go on without us."

It was morning before we wandered back into the castle. This time when we did, I made sure to bring Franklin along. I pulled Grace aside the moment I walked inside.

She knew right away what I meant to ask and agreed even before I spoke. Morna had warned her ahead of time when she sent our invitations through. With permission granted, I presented young Franklin to Cooper. I knew from the way the pup leapt from my arms and into his that the two of them were made for one another.

I stood back watching them wrestle on the floor with a smile in my heart as Orick came up and wrapped his arms around me.

Standing in my husband's arms with friends and family around me, I felt nothing but joy.

For the first time in a long time, I could see past tomorrow. I couldn't wait to see what was yet to come.

Epilogue

Callum wished all of them well, but three nights was enough of a gathering for him.

"Are ye sure ye doona wish to stay only one more night? The rest plan to leave come morning."

Callum appreciated Orick's gesture, but he was ready to return to the Cagair of his own time, return to the quiet halls of his castle.

"Thank ye, but no. I'll see the others when they pass through tomorrow. I'm pleased for ye, that ye've found all that ye have. I'll see ye often, I'm sure."

He embraced Orick and made his way down the stairwell, disappearing from sight with ease.

It took a moment for him to register his surroundings on the other side—the travels had a way of shaking one up.

Smoke reached his nostrils even before he started up the stairwell. Panic surged through him as he worked to climb his way out. Callum burst through the door at the top, gagging and spitting as he ran out onto the grounds of the castle and turned his head up in horror.

Cagair Castle was in flames.

Keep reading for a Sneak Peek of the next book in the series, ***Love Beyond Belief.***

Sneak Peek Of Love Beyond Belief (Book 7 Of Morna's Legacy Series)

PROLOGUE

Cagair Castle—September 1649

Callum could scarcely see through the billowing smoke. The burning in his lungs made it difficult for him to think as he ran across the lawn to better see what all was aflame. Why did it get hotter the further he ran from the castle? He spun to see the source of the heat—Orick's old hut—engulfed, the thatch roof quickly disintegrating, the wood beams creaking as fire consumed them.

Frantic thoughts coursed through his mind until he landed on the one comforting fact he could grasp. None of the servants were there. He sent them all away before leaving to join the celebration with the rest of his family and friends. Thank God for that.

He allowed relief to rush over him until he heard a sound so unsettling that he couldn't believe it possible—the screams of a babe, a young one. The sound of its cries—screeching, pained, and so frightened—chilled Callum's bones even as heat rose around him.

It wasn't real. It couldn't be. He was the only one at the castle. Then he remembered Tom—the old man from the village who always came up to check on things when Callum was away. He hoped Tom was still at home with his family, that he'd come and gone long before the fire took hold. Surely the sound was his imagination. How could a child be here?

He ran to escape the cloud of smoke surrounding him and tripped over an object in his path. He regained his footing and screamed, sucking in enough smoke to make his mind swirl. Tom. Unconscious and stabbed in his abdomen, the man lay bleeding out onto the grass.

The sound. He could hear it again. Screaming. Screaming. Over and over. He had to go see. He had to save the child inside. He couldn't let the smoke overtake him until he saw the babe safe.

In one quick moment of clear thought, he ripped the shirt from his body, tying it quickly over his nose and mouth to block some of the smoke from entering his lungs. Not taking a second longer to ponder his choice, he burst into the burning hut and moved blindly toward the sound of the screams.

He found the child quickly. As he reached for it, he could see the outline of two others, clearly dead not from fire but from smoke. That same deadly threat would most likely take his life in a few short moments. He just hoped he could see the child safely outside and that by some miracle, the babe would live.

He managed to run with the child far outside the smoke before he fell from a sudden pain in his leg. He let loose of the infant, hoping it was far enough from the flames to survive. His leg was on fire, and the pain pushed away any clear thought. He rolled and swung until the fire died around him, but the pain made everything around him spin.

Nothing would stop the fire, save magic, and he wasn't a sorcerer by any stretch.

Unconsciousness threatened him. Whether it was from smoke or pain, he didn't know. Just as he began to give himself over to what he expected was death, rain started to pound upon his face. In panic, he threw himself over the child to keep her from drowning in the water.

Then he saw her—a woman. Old and cloaked she stood there, arms stretched as if she summoned the storm from willpower alone. The fire surrendered, and so did he, closing his eyes as he held the baby against him.

To finish the story, order your copy of *Love Beyond Belief* today.

Read all the books in Morna's Legacy Series:

LOVE BEYOND TIME (BOOK 1)

LOVE BEYOND REASON (BOOK 2)

A CONALL CHRISTMAS (BOOK 2.5)

LOVE BEYOND HOPE (BOOK 3)

LOVE BEYOND MEASURE (BOOK 4)

IN DUE TIME – A NOVELLA (BOOK 4.5)

LOVE BEYOND COMPARE (BOOK 5)

LOVE BEYOND DREAMS (BOOK 6)

LOVE BEYOND BELIEF (BOOK 7)

About The Author

Bethany Claire is the USA Today bestselling author of the Scottish time travel romance novels in Morna's Legacy Series.

Bethany's love of storytelling has been a lifelong passion but, convinced it would serve her best to follow a "conventional" career path, she tucked that passion away and went off to college.

Connect With Me Online

http://www.bethanyclaire.com
http://twitter.com/BClaireAuthor
http://facebook.com/bethanyclaire
http://www.pinterest.com/bclaireauthor

If you enjoyed reading *Love Beyond Compare*, I would appreciate it if you would help others enjoy this book, too.

Recommend it. Help other readers find this book by recommending it to friends, readers' groups and discussion boards.

Review it. Please tell other readers why you like this book by reviewing it at the retailer of your choice. If you do write a review, please send me an email to bclaire@bethanyclaire.com so I can thank you with a personal email, or you can visit my website at http://www.bethanyclaire.com

Join the Bethany Claire Newsletter!

Sign up for my newsletter to receive up-to-date information of books, new releases, events, and promotions.

http://bethanyclaire.com/contact.php#mailing-list

Acknowledgements

My special thanks and gratitude to the following: Karen Corby, Elizabeth Halliday, and Marsha Bredeson—my proofreading team members. Dj Hendrickson—my patient and kind editor. Mom—assistant, therapist, formatter. I couldn't do what I do without each and every one of you. Thank you.

Manufactured by Amazon.ca
Bolton, ON